THE RIVER'S GIFT

Mercedes Lackey

THE RIVER'S GIFT

A ROC BOOK

ROC
Published by New American Library, a division of
Penguin Putnam Inc., 375 Hudson Street, New York, New York 10014, U.S.A.
Penguin Books Ltd, 27 Wrights Lane, London W8 5TZ, England
Penguin Books Australia Ltd, Ringwood, Victoria, Australia
Penguin Books Canada Ltd, 10 Alcorn Avenue, Toronto, Ontario, Canada M4V 3B2
Penguin Books (N.Z.) Ltd, 182–190 Wairau Road, Auckland 10, New Zealand

Penguin Books Ltd, Registered Offices: Harmondsworth, Middlesex, England

First published by Roc, an imprint of New American Library,
a division of Penguin Putnam Inc.

First Printing, October 1999
10 9 8 7 6 5 4 3 2 1

 REGISTERED TRADEMARK—MARCA REGISTRADA

LIBRARY OF CONGRESS CATALOGING-IN-PUBLICATION DATA:
Lackey, Mercedes.
  The river's gift / Mercedes Lackey.
  p. cm.
ISBN 0-451-45759-5
I. Title.
PS3562.A246 R58 1999
813'.54—dc21
                                      99-14509
                                      CIP

Printed in the United States of America

BOOKS ARE AVAILABLE AT QUANTITY DISCOUNTS WHEN USED TO PROMOTE PRODUCTS OR
SERVICES. FOR INFORMATION PLEASE WRITE TO PREMIUM MARKETING DIVISION, PENGUIN
PUTNAM INC., 375 HUDSON STREET, NEW YORK, NEW YORK 10014.

THE RIVER'S GIFT

High above Ariella's head, a mere speck of a lark soared and caroled in the azure sky, its song descending in a sweet rain of silver notes. Beneath her bare feet, soft grass studded with meadowsweet and tiny clover blossoms flowed cool and velvety. Ariella ran mostly for the joy of release, but partly from guilt—if she got out of earshot of the Manor quickly enough, she would be able to say in truth that she hadn't heard Magda calling her.

And inevitably, her chaperone would call, as soon as she realized that Ariella was not at the loom in the solar, at her embroidery frame in her room, or her fine sewing in the garden. Magda was supposed to be educating her—

Except that she doesn't teach me anything that hasn't to do with a needle, Ariella thought with youthful scorn. *Everything I've learned about herbs and simples came from the monks at the Abbey. And everything I've learned about the forest I learned by myself, with no one to teach me. So there!* Magda had become more fretful, more insistent of late that her charge "behave as a proper lady." Perhaps it was the advent of her sixteenth birthday that had brought all this nonsense on—Magda seemed to place great significance on it, though as far as Ariella could see, one more birthday made no difference at all to her. Her Papa treated her the same, the serfs and servants had not changed towards her. Only Magda acted as though sixteen years meant something portentous.

So Ariella ran through the meadow to escape her tormentor, the single-minded old woman who tried to keep her pent up inside the dark, chill manor or confined to the stiflingly manicured garden in the center courtyard. She ran, and she hoped that today she could outrun that unwelcome call of, "Lady Ariella! This is unseemly!"

"Behaving as a proper lady" did not include discarding her hennin headdress and veil, heavily embroidered linen gown, chemise, leather shoes and stockings, donning an old, threadbare, homespun dress and kilting it up above her knees, then running off bare-legged, bare-headed and barefooted to the forest. Proper behavior required too much of one who had run free since she had been able to run at all.

And if a lady could not course through the wild forest surrounding her home, then she did not want to be a lady.

Ariella reached the safety of the forest and ducked beneath an overhanging bough, not even the least out of breath. She paused for a moment among the shadows and peered through a screen of leaves across the meadow to the Manor.

The stone-walled building slumbered behind its moat, with a single sleepy guard standing watch on the wall and a pair of swans gliding undisturbed on the waters. She breathed a shallow sigh. *If luck be with me, Magda is safely asleep, never knowing that I am not where she believes me to be.* If Magda had gone off to take her nap, she'd not awaken until her maidservant came to summon her to the evening meal. By then, Ariella would be safely home, and if there was nothing to show in the way of fine work for the passing of the hours, Magda would only chide her for day-dreaming the time away.

Now that she was safely within the invisible walls of her sylvan sanctuary, Ariella sat down on a drift of last year's leaves and took the time to braid her hair. When she was done, she bound up the end of the shining golden tail, as thick as her wrist and as long as her arm, with a bit of leather thong she fished out of the left-side pocket tied about her waist. Her two pockets bulged with her pilfered stores, and Magda would have had a litter of kittens if she'd known that Ariella frequently ransacked the stillroom to get her treasures.

In her mind she heard Magda's shrill voice, cracking as it always did when the old woman grew agitated. "Those simples are for humans, not the beasts of the field! God have mercy, that I should be cursed with the task of civilizing such a fool of a girl!"

It was hard not to feel resentment towards the old busybody, who grudged every leaf of plantain and drop of cordial as if she and not Ariella had been the one who'd gathered and produced the remedies kept in the stillroom. *I could understand her attitude if she'd been the one working all winter distilling essences and blending tinctures— but surely if I made these things, I should be allowed to decide how to use them!*

Ariella sighed again, this time deeply, as she slipped through the tangle of bushes and briars as easily as a bit

5

of mist, rarely catching so much as a thread of her skirt on a thorn. But after all, she had plenty of practice to learn to move so surely here. That was one thing that Magda could never say, that she was clumsy.

Bringing Magda here to take charge over her had been her father's idea, and a poor one Ariella thought it was. She guessed that it had been in response to that minstrel's distasteful interest not long after she'd turned twelve when her shape had taken on strange new curves and she'd outgrown the bodices of her gowns almost overnight. He'd only tried to kiss her hand, for heaven's sake! Oh, and he'd made moon-calf eyes at her, and sung love-songs at her, but that was hardly anything to fret over. *I haven't needed a nursemaid since I was four, and I don't need one now,* Ariella thought rebelliously, passing crab-wise between two close-growing trees and coming out on a deer-trail. *As if I couldn't take care of myself with a cheeky mountebank! Aye, or anyone else, for that matter!* She knew she'd only to whistle anywhere on the Manor grounds, and no matter where they were, her father's pack of mastiffs would come running to her side, ready to defend her against all threats. Why, not even an armored knight would take his chances against six full-grown mastiffs, much less a silly singer! And for all that she was slender and willow-slim, she was strong, and not the kind of swooning simpleton who wouldn't be willing to pick up a poker or a dagger and defend herself, if it came to that.

Her father's supposed reason for calling his aged cousin Magda out of her retirement in a convent to chaperone his daughter was that he wanted her to learn "manners" and be more "ladylike." Why he should wish such a thing, Ariella had no idea, for she knew as certainly as she knew the sun would rise each day that her Papa had no intention of giving her up in marriage to anyone, no matter how highborn—and she was in full agreement with his plans. Why, how could she ever leave this place, when there was so much that needed tending, her Papa not the least? She had long since learned all there was to know about the proper management of Swan Manor, although since the hiring of the new major domo, there was precious little management she needed to deal with.

If only she could persuade him to send silly Magda away again, she would be perfectly content in every way. *I have the Abbey library, I have Papa, and I have the forest. What more could anyone need?* Oh, she'd heard enough ballads and tales from minstrels and bards to know how a young maiden was supposed to spend her days—dreaming of a romance, sighing after love, waiting for a husband. She didn't have the words to express how much of a waste of time that seemed to her.

She realized that she was all bound up in her annoyance and growing angry, and she stopped dead in her tracks, then, right in the middle of the game-trail. *I have to stop this*, she scolded herself. *I'm going to frighten them off.*

She closed her eyes and cleared her mind, concentrating on the moment and nothing more.

First, the scent of the forest, green and cool, with hints of resin and a waft of old, dead leaves. Then the feel of the trail beneath her feet, soft with leaf-litter. Last, the sounds all around her, the songs of larks and starlings, the chirp of sparrows, the calling of crows and rooks, the trill of wrens, the chattering of squirrels—the rustle of leaves in the breeze—the creak of branches and the snapping of twigs.

When she felt calm and at peace, when all of her annoyance with Magda was gone—that was when she felt the first soft touch on her foot.

She opened her eyes and looked down, and as she expected, there was a young rabbit gazing mournfully up at her, one ear torn and bleeding freely, the marks of sharp teeth visible. At a guess, he had escaped from the jaws of a stoat.

With a bit of waste wool to pad the ear, a bit of soothing ointment, and grass plaited into string to bind it all up, the rabbit was soon on his way. But before she was done with her work, she already had a gathering about her feet of three more patients: a hedgehog with an injured paw, a squirrel with a gashed side, and another rabbit, this one limping with a broken leg.

There were no more small animals waiting for her ministrations when she had finished with these three. She waited to see if any more would appear, but none did, and she walked on until she came to the river, where, by custom, she tended the larger creatures and the hunters.

There was an unvoiced truce among the wounded; she had never seen an injured animal attacked by another in her presence, although she very well knew that many of these creatures would not hesitate a moment to kill and eat each other in different circumstances. She often wondered about that, but nothing she had witnessed had given her an answer.

Magic, she thought with content mingled with wonder. That must be the answer. It felt strange to be in the presence of magic, and stranger still to be the one conjuring it. But it was dangerous too; scores of tales told her how dangerous it was to be known as a witch or a magician.

She heard the river long before she saw it, rushing beyond the screen of the trees, cooling the breeze with its breath. There was a great gray wolf waiting for her by the riverside, and when she approached him—carefully, for experience told her that animals in pain sometimes snapped at her if she startled them—he held his mouth open for her to see the broken, abscessed tooth that must have been causing him agony.

"Oh, you poor thing!" she exclaimed involuntarily, for she had suffered from a similar affliction as a child and knew how much it must hurt. But this case would require more of her "special" talent than usual; animals usually suffered silently beneath her ministrations as she eased pain, but nothing would keep such a dangerous beast quiet as she inflicted more pain than he already suffered. Being bitten while trying to help did not figure into her plans.

Gently, she bent down and she placed one hand on his head, and concentrated all of her thoughts on one thing.

Sleep—

The wolf resisted her at first—it went entirely against his natural instincts to make himself so vulnerable without the protection of the pack around him—but at last, with a sigh, his head drooped, his legs buckled, and he dropped to the ground. She knelt beside him, making certain that he was not going to awaken until she was ready for him to do so. He would not feel what she did to him until she was finished, and then he would have relief instead of nagging pain.

Now she did what she had to—using the small version of a horseshoe-nail-puller she had coaxed the blacksmith into making for her, she clamped the iron jaws about the rotten stump of a tooth, braced the wolf's head between her feet, and pulled. She strained her arms until they hurt, and at last the tooth tore free of the jaw, and pus and blood oozed out.

She had her work cut out for her this time. Only when the tooth was gone, and she had used her magic to reduce the swelling and pain, and the infected socket was cleansed with brandy and packed with bread-mold and spider-webs, did Ariella wake the wolf as gently as she had put him to sleep.

He leapt up from her lap as if he'd been stung, and sped off into the forest without a backward glance. She didn't mind; none of her sylvan patients ever gave any evidence that they felt gratitude for her ministrations. She'd been hurt and disappointed at first, especially in the excitement of learning that her special gift with the animals of the Manor-farm extended to the animals of the forest, but she had gradually come to realize that the fact that they came to her at all was a mark of supreme trust.

After the wolf came a fallow doe, and after the doe, a hawk with a broken talon, and a wildcat with sick kittens. As the cat left, her kittens feeling well enough now to frisk behind her, Ariella dangled her feet in the cool water and gazed out on the river, a sense of lassitude and content coming over her.

Only one person in the entire Manor knew of her abilities, the mute and half-witted dog-boy who cosseted, fed, tended, and slept with his charges, for the dogs were the first who had come to her to be cured. She was wise enough not to be caught by anyone else; she might have gotten by, dosing the animals with herbs, but if anyone had ever seen her heal illnesses and injuries by touch alone, as she had with the hawk and the kittens—then she could find herself in a great deal of difficulty.

Such healings made her tired and sleepy, however, and it

was good to rest against the trunk of a willow with her feet in the water, and watch sun-dazzle dancing over the surface.

She was half-asleep, and thought it was a dream, when the slick-shining, handsome black stallion rose out of the river before her and moved into the shallows to stand at her feet, tossing his head impatiently.

She studied him dreamily as he waded through the sparkling water towards her, diamond-drops falling from his streaming mane and tail and rolling down his heaving sides. His nostrils flared nervously, and he vibrated with suppressed energy. So dark it was blue-black, his satin coat gleamed, highlighted by more gem-drops of water. She gazed at him without moving, unwilling to break the dream, until he shoved her leg impatiently with his nose, making it clear that this was no dream.

With a squeak of surprise, she jumped up. The stallion still stood before her, hock-deep in the water, glaring at her with furious scarlet eyes. He tossed his head and trumpeted an angry call that rang and echoed up and down the river, startling the birds in the tree above her into explosive flight.

This was no farm-horse, strayed this way by accident. This stallion was wild—full of rage—and dangerous.

She tried to touch him with her thoughts, to soothe him as she had so many other wild, pain-maddened creatures—and met a barrier as implacable as the stone walls of the Manor.

Met it? That was too tame—she slammed into it abruptly, leaving her as dazed for a moment as if she had run headlong into a rock cliff.

She shook her head, trying to clear it, as she clutched the trunk of the tree beside her to keep from falling. When she could see again, she stared into those half-mad eyes and swallowed.

A startled thought flashed through her mind. *This isn't just a horse—*

:Of course I'm not a horse, foolish little mortal child,: a strange and imperious voice snarled inside her head, making her start again. *:Now get your wits about you and help me!:*

"Help you?" she replied faintly. "How?"

For answer, the stallion raised his left forefoot out of the water. In shocking contrast to his stunning perfection, that foot was swollen to three times its normal size.

There were times when hurt or sickness seized her; impelled her past her fear, past her ability to think, forcing her to reach out and heal. She had no choice at those times—and this was one of them, in spite of the fact that memory had supplied sudden and frightening recognition of the creature before her.

As the stallion had said, he was no horse. He was a riverhorse, a Kelpie, and deadly to humans. By all reports, Kelpies hated mortals, and would do anything to rid the forest of them. If he'd had a choice, she would not be standing before him now, she would be drowning in the fastest part of the river, lured there by his own magic.

Be sensible! she told herself sharply. *If he wants help, he isn't going to hurt you, is he?*

As if she had any choice—her power responded to his own magic and need in a way that overwhelmed her conscious reservations.

Before the Kelpie had the opportunity to react, she reached out against her own will and grasped the injured forefoot, and quick examination by touch proved that the Kelpie was no different than an ordinary horse, in this at least. There was a hard object lodged between the frog and the hoof, much as a stone would have been, except that this didn't feel like a stone and had caused far more swelling than she would have expected. Encouraged by the Kelpie's statuelike immobility, she waded into the water so that she could turn the bottom of the hoof upward. It was then that she saw the nature of the object—an iron horseshoe nail.

There was only one way to get that out. She reached into her pocket for the nail-puller.

But the moment she brought it out, the Kelpie reared back, water splashing wildly as he lashed out with his good hoof, ears flattened back and teeth bared. *:No more Cold Iron!:* he shouted in her mind.

And that I can't blame him for—if a single nail has caused him such pain and hurt.

But she stood her ground, hands on her hips. "If you want that nail out, I have to use this," she snapped back, brandishing the nail-puller at him. He shied back, eyes rolling, and stayed away from the tool. "I can't get that nail out otherwise!" she insisted. "I'll try not to touch you with it, but I can't help you without it!"

She knew why he was afraid of the tool—and why his forefoot was so swollen and inflamed from a mere scrap of metal. Cold Iron was deadly to the creatures of Faerie, and the bit of nail would likely kill him unless he could find someone to get it out. But the only creature that could, would perforce be a mortal, like herself—potentially just as deadly an enemy to him as he was to mortals.

He finally calmed somewhat and took a few limping steps towards her, his neck stretched out, his ears still flattened back. *:Swear! Swear you won't touch me with that thing!:* he demanded.

She sighed, but swore as he demanded, and at length he allowed her to take his fore-hoof in her hand again, set the nail-puller carefully onto the head of the nail, and begin working.

She was no blacksmith, to accomplish the task in a single pull. She had only the strength of any other young girl, and the only way she could get the nail out was to wriggle the nasty thing back and forth, pulling all the while, getting it loose by infinitesimal degrees. Both she and the Kelpie were exhausted and sweating by the time she worked the nail free and dropped it into her pocket.

But she was not so exhausted that she forgot to weave her spell of healing about the hoof.

As soon as she let the Kelpie go, he danced backwards, throwing his head to the side as he curveted out of her reach. She expected him to vanish as the wild animals did, but instead he paused, injured foot raised out of the water, and turned to stare at her.

Already the hoof was nearly normal size again, and she wondered what he thought he was going to do now. Other than charge her—and she did have the nail-puller to defend herself with—he couldn't hurt her. She already knew what he was; he could not possibly beguile her onto his back so that he could carry her off to drown her. Was it possible that he was grateful? A creature of Faerie, purportedly with neither heart nor soul?

He took another step towards her, his head down. *:You helped me, mortal child. You didn't have to, you could have chased me away, but you helped me even though I was rude and angry. Why?:*

21

She didn't really know the answer to that herself, so she shrugged. "I suppose because you were in pain and needed help," she replied. She thought for a moment, then added, tentatively, "You didn't ask to get an iron nail in your foot. The stories about your kind aren't very—flattering, but as far as you doing anything, I haven't heard of anyone being drowned in this river by a Kelpie. . . ."

The Kelpie nickered, clearly laughing at her. *:I prefer to frighten the silly fools. Drowning them would taint the water, mortal child.:*

She reflected that anyone who saw a magnificent black stallion running loose would know her Papa had no such animal and leave it alone, recognizing the Kelpie for what it was, or would be a thief who deserved what he got for trying to steal a valuable animal.

"I wish you'd stop calling me 'mortal child,'" she added with a touch of irritation. "How would you like it if I called you 'soulless demon'? My name is Ariella."

The Kelpie stepped back a pace, his ears going straight up with surprise, and she recalled that names were supposed to give magical creatures power over each other. Well, nothing to be done now.

:My name—: he began hesitantly, *:You can call me Merod.:*

It probably wasn't his "real" name, but it was one he would answer to, and that was good enough. "I'm glad I was able to help you, Merod," she said with a decided little nod. "And if you feel any obligation towards me for that help, you can discharge it simply by not drowning anyone from Swan Manor."

He nickered again, green eyes flashing with mischief. *:That's a poor bargain for you, asking me to do only what I would be inclined to do anyway, Ariella.:*

"And I hardly have the means to compel you to do anything, do I?" she countered as he tossed his head with merriment. "And honestly, I have everything I need or want right here in the forest."

He pawed the water, sending sparkling drops flying in every direction, then whirled on his heels and dashed into the deepest part of the river, vanishing beneath the rippling water. She stared after him, then laughed breathlessly.

A Kelpie! She had seen, touched, spoken with a real creature of magic! She hugged her arms to her chest as if she clasped the secret to her. From this moment on, nothing would ever be the same.

The odious Magda was nowhere to be seen when she slipped back into the Manor. Thankful, she went directly to her sun-filled room and hurriedly changed out of her woods-running clothes. With great regret, she dusted the last traces of the forest off herself and put on the silken hose, the leather slippers, the fine, white linen chemise, and the heavy amber gown with its train and encumbering folds of wide skirt. With a sigh, she tucked her hair into a net and adjusted her linen veil over it, then donned the jangling chatelaine belt that Magda insisted she wear. Her "real" clothing went back into the chest at the foot of her bed, hidden under her outgrown gowns and linens.

She seated herself at her embroidery frame in the window-seat overlooking the garden-court and picked up her needle just in time; she hadn't taken more than three stitches when puffing and shuffling from the room next to hers signaled that Lady Magda had finally arisen from her nap.

Ariella shook her head, as the next few moments brought the querulous call of "Ariella? Ariella? Where are you, child?"

"At my frame, Lady Magda," Ariella called back, and she waited for Lady Magda to make her stately appearance.

The round-topped wooden door squeaked open, and Magda moved ponderously into Ariella's brightly lit room, squinting at the light. "Child, are you sitting in the sunlight again? You'll spoil your complexion, I've told you a hundred times! And you'll fade your work."

Since Ariella didn't particularly care whether the altar-cloth she was working on was ever finished, much less if the colors were faded, she held her tongue.

Lady Magda looked nothing like her cousin, Ariella's father; where Ariella's Papa was thin and dark, Lady Magda was plump and florid, of no more than middling height, with squinting, short-sighted blue eyes and a mouth like a pinched-up purse. Although she had not taken holy orders and apparently had no intention of doing so, she always dressed in nunlike gray, black, and white, heavy gowns which were far from comfortable in the heat of summer, so that her face was always red and damp with perspiration.

The Lady moved ponderously into Ariella's room, her eyes shaded with one hand against the sunlight. She cast a critical eye on Ariella's indifferent sewing and made a *tsk*ing sound. "Next to nothing done, as usual! I suppose you've been daydreaming again! Well, let me hear you recite your lesson."

Ariella would have preferred lessons in history, Greek, or mathematics, but Lady Magda's learning was not in any of those fields. Her "lesson" was the next in an interminable number of saints' lives which Ariella was to learn by heart each day. Since these pious bits of prose were hardly complicated, varying only in the details of how each saint met his or her (usually spectacularly painful and gory) end, it was quite easy for Ariella to rattle her day's lesson off to Lady Magda's reluctant satisfaction without ever having to put much effort into learning it.

The Lady sniffed as Ariella finished, and she shook

her head. "At least no one can claim you are ignorant!" she said plaintively. "Though what a well-bred lady would make of your needle-skills, I'm at a loss to say! Off with you, child. Pray bring your Papa to the hall; it's almost time to dine."

Ariella gladly left her embroidery frame and flew across the room to the door as Lady Magda bleated, "And don't run! A lady does not run!" quite uselessly behind her.

Her Papa would be in his study, working with his steward. He took care with even the smallest details of the needs of his small-holders and serfs and the crops and beasts they raised for him. If someone had a sick child, he knew about it and had sent to learn if the family needed anything. If someone suffered a blight, then the portion that came to the Manor was reduced or eliminated for that year. And as a result, in a good year, no one begrudged the Lord his share, and often little additional gifts in the way of flowers and herbs, game, nuts, or wild berries found their way to the Manor's kitchens.

Lord Kaelin and his steward were just closing up the great books in which all the accounts and doings of the Manor were recorded when Ariella presented herself at his door, not the least out of breath. Lord Kaelin turned at the sound of her light footstep, smiling and holding out his hand.

"My Wild Swan!" he exclaimed fondly, as he always did. "Come to make certain I eat, eh?"

The steward smiled, and slipped out of the room without saying anything, as Ariella seized her father's hand and kissed it, then cuddled into his embrace. "Of course, Papa," she replied as he stroked her hair. "If I don't come to remind you, you'll spend all day in this dark little hole!" She lowered her voice. "Papa," she continued plaintively, "can't we send Lady Magda home? She doesn't teach me anything that the Abbot couldn't. And the Abbot has more learning than she does."

"But the Abbot cannot teach you the skills of a lady—" Lord Kaelin began.

"Nor do I need them!" she replied instantly. "I've no intention of ever leaving Swan Manor and you."

Her father simply shook his head and rose to his feet. "We'd best be getting down to the great hall," was all he said, and she knew that once again she had lost this particular argument.

The next day, when she returned to the forest, she wondered if she would see the Kelpie again and was a little disappointed when she reached the riverbank and he did not appear. But when she had finished with the last of her large patients, she felt a tugging at the hem of her skirt.

When she looked to see what it was, she got something of a shock. Holding on to her hem was the oddest little creature she had ever seen in her life. It looked rather like a little man, and rather like a tangle of ancient briar root, all clothed in a patchwork garment made of leaves carefully stitched together.

The little creature pulled off his hat when he saw he'd gotten her attention, and then he coughed. It was a nasty sound, indeed, and she immediately knew it wasn't a healthy cough.

"If ye please, mum," the little man said hoarsely. "If ye'd be havin' anythin'—"

"Of course!" she replied, instinctively dropping down into a crouch so that her face was level with his. She fished out her packets of herbs and made up two sets, tying them up in two large leaves with a bit of grass. "Here," she said, handing him the first, done up in plaintain. "You take this, put it in boiling water, and breathe the steam as often as you can. Then you take this"—she handed him a packet done up in a dock leaf—"and you make tea with it, and drink it with lots of honey. Wrap up in wool and keep yourself very warm, and if the cough hasn't gone off in three or four days, come back and see me."

The little man's gnarled, brown face was flushed with gratitude. "Thenkee, mum," he said, and then—vanished. She hadn't even blinked her eyes, and he was gone.

She stood up, slowly, and turned when she heard something like a chuckle behind her.

There stood Merod, coat shining blue-black in a shaft of sunlight driving down through the tree-canopy. *:He won't be the last of your patients, mor— Ariella,:* the Kelpie said in her mind. *:They trust you now.:*

"Because I didn't hurt you?" she asked, settling herself on the riverbank and dangling her feet in the cool water.

:Because you kept your word,: Merod corrected her. *:And now both Underhill and Overhill are open to you. Now you may*

32

come and go, and look and know, and no door shall be locked against you.:

So it proved, as the summer days passed and Ariella found herself playing physician to a bewildering variety of uncanny creatures. She splinted broken bones, treated wounds, and dosed fevers. She tended odd little babies, in cradles that looked to have been grown rather than carved, for croup and colic and all the little ailments that made human babies fretful. She learned that when you tend to a tree-spirit, you must also tend to her tree; that an otter-maid is as full of mischief as a "natural" otter; and that a sylph could only take in medicine through the air. All of her charges healed with unbelievable swiftness, and it wasn't often that she needed to use her magical powers to mend them, for they had a touch of that gift themselves. It was only when the hurt was caused by the hand of man—usually due to the touch or presence of iron—that she had to exert that touch of healing to set things right.

Over the course of time, Merod thawed, and soon they were true friends. Indeed, she had never had a real friend, for there were no young people of her own age and rank anywhere near Swan Manor, and Lady Magda would not consent to let her even speak with those below her, as she used to do when she was a child. Of course, all the young people of her age were far too busy working in the gardens and fields, tending flocks and herds, and hard at labor at loom, dairy, kitchen, or elsewhere to have any time for friendship with Lord Kaelin's daughter. She had not realized how lonely she was until she met Merod, who seemed to be the tacit leader of all of the Faerie hereabouts.

There were none of the Great Ones of Faerie present in her forest, somewhat to her disappointment; according to Merod, there was too much Cold Iron about for them to be comfortable, so she never saw any of the tall, proud, and fearfully beautiful Elvenkind. But the lesser spirits were here in abundance.

:It is because your father treats the land with kindness, and he is generous and thoughtful,: Merod told her as they strolled together along the bank of the river one sunny day. *:And he treats his people with kindness. They are happy, the land is happy and healthy, and we can flourish. Other places are not so good for us.:*

"How is that?" she asked.

:Where there is greed and misery, such dark thoughts drive us away—and sometimes open the doors of Underhill to the Dark Faerie.: Merod wouldn't say anything more than that, but she didn't need him to elaborate. She had heard enough tales, both from traveling musicians and from the people of the Manor, to know what he was talking about. The worst that Merod's kind ever in-

dulged in was a bit of mischief, throwing a bit of a fright into someone who deserved it. But there were others—the Kelpies who did drown wayfarers, the Night Hags, the Willowisps that lured the lost into bogs to perish, a hundred and one other nasty creatures who seemed to live only to cause misery and death. If Merod was to be believed—and he'd been truthful with her up to now—the presence of these creatures was due as much to the ill-doing of humans as it was to their own will and desires.

That was certainly cause for some uneasy thoughts. Were mortals as much the cause of their own misfortune as all that? It made her feel obscurely guilty.

"Have you ever seen any of the Great Ones?" she asked, to turn her mind elsewhere.

He laughed. *:Of course! I have been here far longer than your kind. Long before sheep ever grazed on the Downs, the Great Ones came to this river to bathe and hold revels. I would*

*take them for rides beneath the waves—they cannot drown, of
course, and they thought it fine sport. And one day, one of them
even gave me a gift. Shall I show it to you?:*

She flushed with excitement. "Oh yes! Please!"

He plunged into the water and soon returned bearing
a green silk pouch in his teeth. *:Open it,:* he urged, placing it in her hand. She obeyed, and three transparent
spheres, filled with a rainbow mist, as fragile as bubbles,
rolled into her hand.

She gazed at them, half afraid to touch them with her
fingers.

*:You can't hurt them, they won't break, not until I want them
to,:* Merod told her, and emboldened, she rolled them in
her hand and held them up to the light, entranced by the
opalescent colors that played inside.

"What are they?" she asked.

:Wishes—of a kind,: Merod told her. *:The Great Faerie
never give anything without conditions attached, and they are*

inclined to twist everything into a riddle. I haven't the faintest idea why I was given these in the first place. The Great One told me that I might want them one day—but that the first one would make me mortal, and the other two had to be shared.: He tossed his head and snickered. *:I've never seen a reason to want to be mortal, and I doubt I ever will, so they're really rather useless. I have magic enough for everything I need!:*

"That's certainly true," Ariella agreed, rolling the spheres back into their pouch and handing it back to him. "I'm sure I wouldn't know what to do with them. But they're lovely to look at."

:That's why I keep them, instead of giving them to one of the nixies to play with,: he told her, and he plunged back into the river to replace his treasures in their hiding-place.

She continued to walk slowly along the bank, knowing that he would come out of the water beside her wherever she went.

:By the way,: Merod said, emerging again from the river

and resuming the conversation as if it had never been interrupted, *:why were you so late today?:*

Ariella made a face. "Lady Magda got it into her head that if she worked on that stupid altar-cloth with me, I'd probably make more progress, so I had to sit there sewing until she began to yawn and couldn't keep her eyes open anymore."

Merod stopped, and she turned to look at him.

:You know, I've never understood why you waste your time with that nonsense when you're needed elsewhere. The other mortals here need your healing, too—why do you spend hours making patterns in thread?:

"Because Lady Magda says—" she began.

:Is it wrong to help others?: Merod asked.

"Well—no." Ariella fidgeted uneasily, for Merod had put his finger—well, hoof—on exactly what bothered her the most about Lady Magda's decrees. For some time now, she had wanted to offer her healing skills to the folk of the Manor, but Lady Magda absolutely forbade her to "mingle" with the common people except at harvest, when every hand was needed, hers included. "No, and it seems to me that it's really wrong to be spending time on such foolery and fripperies when there are people who need help."

:Has this woman power over you? Can she compel you to remain indoors? Or is it only that you fear her disapproval?:

Ariella grimaced. "She'd tell Papa—" she began, then shook her head. "If I was just running off to play in the forest, it would be different, but I can't see how Papa would be angry if I were helping the sick." She raised her head and looked Merod straight in his wicked green eyes. "I see what you're thinking. And you're right. It's time I stood up for myself."

He tossed his head, and drops of water flicked off his mane; she could tell he was pleased. *:You're becoming less like a silly mortal maiden and more like one of us every day,:*

was all he said, then he did something he had never done before. He reached out and touched her cheek with his soft nose, exactly like a kiss, and she felt a tingling, a warm thrill pass through her. He pulled back shyly, and she put her hand to her cheek, and neither of them said a word about the moment—but all the way home that evening, she kept putting her hand to the spot on her cheek where he had touched her in a kind of wonder.

The next day, when the lesson had been recited and Lady Magda announced that she and Ariella were going to work on the altar-cloth, Ariella shook her head.

"Not today, Magda," she said carefully, trying to make certain that her tone remained polite. Without another word, she went straight to the carved wooden chest at the foot of her bed and took out her old clothing, laying it on the bed.

"What do you mean—" Magda began. She blinked at the sight of the old dress. "Lady Ariella! Where did you get that rag? Give it to me at once, and I'll take it to—"

"These are my working clothes, Magda," Ariella said levelly. "I can hardly go among the workers to tend to their ills dressed in a fine gown, now, can I?"

"Go among—but—how—" Magda's face grew as red as a ripe apple as she struggled to express herself through her surprise and outrage. Ariella simply went about her business, changing swiftly out of her fine gown and into her comfortable dress, though as a concession to Magda she did slip on a pair of old pattens over her bare feet.

She half thought that Magda might try to push herself between Ariella and the door, but instead the woman sat abruptly down on the edge of the bed, still struggling to make her feelings known. Ariella strode firmly out the door, ignoring Magda's splutterings.

Nor was that all; she went openly to the stillroom and

made up a proper basket of medicines and remedies, thinking that if she was going to defy Lady Magda, she might as well do so properly.

Thus armed, she went down to the village and to each and every tiny earthen-floored home, looking for anyone who might be ill or injured. She was greeted with astonishment and open mouths, but not a one of the people to whom she offered her help turned her down. She found there pretty much the same sorts of ailments that she had been treating in the forest: babies with sour stomachs or nagging coughs, grannies with aching bones, children and adults with sprains, nasty cuts, and a broken bone or two. All her practice on the forest creatures stood her in good stead now, and she was glad of it, for she didn't think she dared exert her healing touch on fellow humans, at least not yet. Before she had gotten half through the village, some of those who had been working out in the fields and sheds came trickling in with minor hurts, probably summoned by children carrying the astonishing news that "the Lady" had come to tend to them.

As she bound up the last of the sprains, she looked about only to find herself surrounded by curious onlookers in their dusty, earth-colored, threadbare working clothes. But the work-worn faces around her showed no sign of fear or animosity, only puzzlement and gratitude. She stood up and straightened her shoulders, and with a nod, addressed a stoop-shouldered old man who she instinctively felt was probably considered to be a leader here. He looked her fearlessly in the face.

"Thenkee, milady," he said humbly. "Th' last hand t' tend us thuslike was yer blessed Lady-Mother. 'Tis far fer us t'be goin' t' the Abbey fer sprains an' belike—"

"Then it's high time I took Mother's place, isn't it? If you like, Uncle," she said, giving him the title that the serfs used with a man they respected, "I'll come every day from now on to see to the village—and beyond, if you'll spread the word. It would be easier for me, if it's possible that everyone beholden to Lord Kaelin were to come here for tending."

"Aye, that," the old man agreed happily. Ariella gathered up what was left of her bandages and medicines and the crowd parted to let her through. She pondered what the old man had told her as she took the path to the Manor that would lead her through the forest.

I never knew that Mother took care of our people. I wonder why Papa never told me? It couldn't have been because he didn't approve; he himself mingled with his serfs and underlings. Perhaps he had simply forgotten, or perhaps Lady Magda had taken it upon herself to pronounce that such a task was "unsuitable" to Ariella's rank, sex, and youth, and Lord Kaelin did not have the fortitude to nay-say her.

That gave her cause to wonder if her mother had also had the gift of magic healing. Or if she'd had it, but had never known and never used it. *After all, I never would have known if the dogs hadn't come to me first, and I didn't know any better and I couldn't help myself. . . .* If her mother had never shared that experience, by the time she had come to Swan Manor as an adult bride, she would probably have ignored the persistent proddings of the power inside her.

She was so sunk in her own thoughts that she hardly noticed when she reached the heart of the forest. It was only when she nearly tripped over a young rabbit that she realized her goal and it was time to begin her ministrations all over again.

Lady Magda was so taken aback by Ariella's rebellion that she did not even trouble herself to challenge Ariella the next day when the girl changed into her old linen dress and marched confidently out to what she now considered to be her duty. She simply shook her head in disbelief and took to her bed for her daily nap. Lord Kaelin said nothing to his daughter about her self- appointed position, and Ariella did not bring the subject up; even if he disapproved as much as Lady Magda did (which she privately doubted) as long as he didn't say anything, she could go right on.

The one creature who did express his approval with a whole heart was Merod. The Kelpie made no secret of how he felt. *:Everything you do to make the other mortals well and happy will make our lives better,:* he declared, switching his tail vigorously. *:If they are well, they will be kinder to the land and the wild things. They will keep their Cold Iron within the bounds of the fields they know. They will not come hunting us, believing that their ills come from our curses.:*

He was in a mischievous and cheerful mood today, frisking coltishly in the shallows. He splashed her, and laughing, she returned the favor, kicking water at him.

:Would you like to see some magic?: he asked her abruptly. None of the other creatures of Faerie had ever made her such an offer, and she inhaled sharply.

"Yes!" she exclaimed before he could change his mind. "All I've ever seen is when one of your friends vanishes—"

:All you haven't seen, you mean,: he snickered, and she reached down to splash him again. *:What makes you think a little water will bother me?:*

"Nothing, obviously." She laughed. "But are you really going to show me something magic?"

:Certainly. Would you care to see what your mother looked like when she first came to Swan Manor?: Without waiting for her reply—which was just as well, since she suddenly felt as if she couldn't breathe—he turned to face the river and pawed the surface of the water three times.

A sparkling mist gathered above the river, fog mingled with streamers of thousands of tiny motes that glittered with jewel-bright, ever-changing colors. The fog thickened, obscuring the other bank; the motes danced and glimmered, dazzling her eyes. Then, all in a single moment, the colors flared and vanished, and hanging in the mist was a vision of a young woman, looking as alive and real as Ariella herself.

The slender maiden stood in quiet attentiveness, head bare of veil, looking up at something. Her hair fell to her knees in two thick plaits, as golden and luxuriant as Ariella's own. Her wide sky-blue eyes gazed upwards with an expression of intense concentration, yet there was a merry sparkle in them, and more than a hint that she would laugh more often than she frowned. The body beneath her blue woolen gown was slender, her neck long and graceful, her hands slim and so white even Lady Magda would have approved. She was very beautiful, and Ariella gazed at her with mingled admiration and doubt.

:You're very like her,: the Kelpie said.

She shook her head. "No, I could never be that beautiful, that graceful. I'm as ungainly as a young calf." The maiden in the Kelpie's vision was as ethereal as an angel, and Ariella could not imagine anyone more unlike her than her daughter. Was this how Lady Magda wanted her to appear? If so, there was little wonder that Lady Magda was so disappointed in her charge.

"I can see now why Papa never wanted to remarry," she said softly. "What other woman could ever compare with my mother?"

:Oh, I suppose there must be some, somewhere,: the Kelpie replied lightly, and shook his head so that his mane flew. The vision of the young woman broke apart into the myriad of sparkling motes. Ariella did not entirely regret losing sight of the woman who had given birth to her. Such a vision of perfection made her all too aware of her own shortcomings.

:You wanted to know what one of the Great Ones look like,: Merod continued. *:Well, here is a gathering of some.:*

This time the motes reformed into not one but several figures, engaged in a stately dance, and Ariella gasped in purest wonder.

They were tall, nothing like the little creatures who came to her to have their ailments tended. Even the sylphs and nixies, the most humanlike of the lot, were never bigger than a tall child of twelve or thirteen. But these beings, even the three females, were taller even than her Papa.

She had thought that her mother was angelic in her perfect beauty; now she swiftly revised her opinion. Her mother had been lovely, but all six of the Faerie possessed an incandescent beauty that scorched the heart and soul and left the mind bedazzled. Their faces were alight with it, their wand-slim figures lithe with it. The men and women alike wore their ebony or silver-gilt hair long, in elaborate arrangements threaded with beads and gems, entwined with thin silver chains, arranged on crystal combs, adorned with wreaths of enormous, pale flowers and silken ribbons. Their garments were like nothing Ariella had ever seen, made of the thinnest gossamer silks, rich with needlework, fluttering with butterfly sleeves, trailing intricately embroidered trains, and embellished with ornaments of silver, gems, and delicate lace. Winglike eyebrows graced elongated emerald eyes, thin and aquiline noses complimented delicate mouths as soft as rose-petals. They moved like swans on the water, swallows in the sky, fish in the deep; like a sigh, like a song. She was obscurely glad that there was no music to accompany their dancing; it would have been too heart-breakingly beautiful for any mere mortal to have borne.

She looked away, unable to bear with so much wonder. When she looked back, the figures were gone, the mist dispersing, and she turned to meet the Kelpie's knowing green eyes.

:Lovely, aren't they? But they are too high for me. I prefer the

beauties of the middle Earth for myself,: was all Merod said, but Ariella knew that he understood.

The days passed, much alike, but too full of enjoyment for Ariella ever to be bored with her lot. So long as the sun shone and the weather was fine, six days out of the week her schedule was much the same. In the mornings Ariella studied what Lady Magda set her, recited yet another saint's life, and took a few stitches on her altar-cloth, feeling that she should at least make a token effort in Lady Magda's direction. As soon as she was able, she freed herself of her encumbering gowns and the formal nonsense Lady Magda thought so important and left "Lady Ariella" behind.

She didn't see the creatures of Faerie every day; in fact she usually didn't see any of them but Merod more than once or twice in a fortnight, if one of them needed her tending. But now that she knew they were all around her, she sensed their invisible presence and often thought she heard them going about their lives in the woods around her.

Merod, however, was a constant friend and companion, and he traded tales of life among the Faerie for her own stories gleaned from the histories and chronicles in the library of the Abbey. He had a lively curiosity about the world outside the forest and was as eager for such stories as a child.

On the rare occasions when it rained during the day, she took her horse and rode to the Abbey to delve among the books or absorb more knowledge of herbs and physik from the Infirmarian and his helpers. When it rained, it was no use going out to the forest; the animals kept to their dens, and Merod had no place for her to take shelter. Besides, rain made the Kelpie wild and restless and not much good as a conversationalist.

And once each week on Sunday, rain or shine, she and

her father rode out together, with Lady Magda trundled along in a horse-litter, to attend holy services at the Abbey chapel.

So the summer passed. Then, before she quite realized it, the summer was gone and the busy season of harvest was upon them. The summer had been perfect for growing, and it seemed that there was an abundance, even an overabundance, everywhere Ariella looked. And while this meant great things for the continued prosperity of Swan Manor and those that depended on the harvest, Ariella knew that until the last fruit was picked and nut gathered in, she would bid farewell to her days of relative leisure. Every hand was needed for such a rich harvest-season, and even Lady Magda would not be spared. The reapers had already been out in the first hay-field, and it was time for all the Manor-folk to set to.

"We start haying tomorrow," she sighed to Merod after

one of the swimming lessons he had insisted on. He was determined that she learn to swim, and swim well, after being taken unaware by the current and getting a fright and a lung-full of water. Now she swam, if not as well as one of the otter-maidens, at least well enough to keep herself out of trouble. She usually stripped to her short chemise to swim, having no fear that any humans would come this way without warning, and feeling no embarrassment in Merod's presence.

Now she combed out her hair with her fingers to help it dry as she sat in a patch of sun, with Merod reclining at his ease beside her, and reluctantly broached the subject of the upcoming harvests and her inevitable absence until they were over. Would Merod be angry with her? Would he feel betrayed? She didn't want to hurt his feelings, but she did have her duty to the Manor—

:So you'll have your hands full for some time, I expect. If we need your skills, we'll find a way to let you know,: the Kelpie

replied matter-of-factly. *:I'll miss your company, of course, but—:* he cocked his head to the side. *:Why are you looking at me so oddly?:*

"How did you know I would have to help with the harvest?" she asked, feeling her eyes widen with surprise.

He laughed. *:I have seen more than three hundred harvests come and go. Do you think I wouldn't recognize the signs of an especially good one? And of course, if the harvest is good, your father will have hired extra hands at the hiring fair and still you and every person in the Manor will need to add your labor.:*

She echoed his laughter. "Of course. I keep forgetting you are as old as the hills themselves," she replied teasingly.

:Not quite as old as the hills, but old enough.: He gave her another of those brief, feather-light touches to the cheek with his nose, so close to a kiss that they gave her chills. *:Go in good conscience and do your duty. I'll miss you, but remember what I've told you.:*

57

He didn't need to repeat it; anything she did to add to the peace and happiness of the lands about the Manor made a difference in the lives of the Faerie folk. So when she made her way back from the forest for what she knew would be the last time for many days, she had the comfort of knowing that though she would sacrifice a little freedom, she would still be adding to the peace of her friends.

The hay was the first of the crops to be gathered in, and it needed a steady space of at least a week with hot sun, no rain, and little dew, for once it was cut, it had to cure before it could be brought into the barns. First the reapers made their way down the fields like an advancing army, sweeping at the succulent grasses with their scythes and leaving the green stems flat on the ground behind them like a vanquished army. Every harvest—though thankfully, never at Swan Manor—reapers lost limbs and lives to a careless swipe of the blades. A good hand with a scythe was worth any three common laborers, and Lord Kaelin rewarded his reapers well.

It was the job of the less skilled to come along behind them and rake the hay into neat rows for the turning, while the harvesters moved across the fields with the precision of clockwork, stopping only to sharpen their instruments. In fields already harvested, where the hay had sufficiently dried, the hay-wains lumbered, with their own crews of rakers, forkers (who tossed clumps of hay up onto the wagons), loaders, and a driver. The hot, still air was full of the sounds of insects buzzing, the reapers chanting, the rakers humming, and the sweet scent of newly mown hay. All of this was thirsty work, and Ariella and Lady Magda labored up and down the rows with the old women and small children with their buckets of cool water. For once Lady Magda eschewed her heavy black and gray gowns for a simple linen chemise and apron, bundling her hair up beneath a kerchief and leaving her dignity back in the Manor.

When the hay was in, it was time for the grain—oats, wheat, barley and rye—all three scythed and harvested in much the same manner as the hay. The weather remained perfect, hot and still, and the golden grain fell before the scythes, rich with the promise of the well-fed winter.

From the fields, the wains went to the threshing circles, where threshers beat the sheaves to loosen the grain from the straw. Ariella worked with the winnowers, tossing basketfuls of grain into the air for the breeze to carry away the lighter chaff while the grain dropped back to the ground.

The harvest wasn't over yet—in fact it was just begun. Next came peas, beans, and other vegetables that would be dried for winter preservation. Ariella was out in the rows with the other women and children, filling her apron with pods and emptying it in the barrow a boy brought up. After the beans and peas came the root vegetables, turnips and mangle-wurzles, beets, onions, and leeks. Then came the hops, then the berries, apples and nuts. Nor was this the end; rushes had to be cut and dried for strewing on the floors, herbs gathered and hung to dry, honey gathered from the hives. Not even the blossoms were spared the gathering-in; lavender, roses and other flowers were stripped of their petals or preserved whole for sweet-scented sachets and potpourris or to be candied, and all of this needed people's hands, Ariella's among them. She worked from the first light of false dawn to the last hint of twilight, fell into her bed exhausted, and woke to do it all over again. Every bucket of grain, every round, white turnip, every apple and honeycomb meant a pleasant and comfortable winter for the people of Swan Manor. No one would go hungry, and there would be extra to sell for things the Manor didn't produce for itself, and still more to sell for luxuries— spices and cakes of white sugar for cooking, oranges to

61

stick full of cloves and hang to scent the air, silks for gowns, dye-stuff—Twelfth-Night gifts. . . .

Ariella indulged herself with imagining what she might buy from peddlers at the Harvest Fair as she worked, sweat dripping down her neck and even off the tip of her nose. And all the while, in the last field of barley to be mowed, a single uncut sheaf stood in the very middle, a sheaf that would be left untouched until the very last apple and nut of the harvest was gathered in.

Finally, at long last, in the final honey-gold moments of an autumn afternoon, the entire population of the Manor gathered behind Lord Kaelin and the chief reaper, each of whom had tiny silver sickles in their hands. Everyone was dressed in his or her best, and even the poorest wore a bright ribbon or two and a wreath of flowers in their hair. Ariella, like the other unmarried maidens, wore her hair unbound and streaming down her back, with a wreath of flowers, wheat, and ribbons crowning her head.

In a body, they all paraded into the fields, singing to the Corn Maiden, for they had come to bring her in.

With great ceremony, Lord Kaelin and Toby, the chief reaper, took careful hold of the last sheaf and bent to cut the stalks off as near to the ground as they could. When the sheaf was cut, they handed it to Toby's wife and Ariella, who swiftly bound it up and made it into a humanlike shape. With bits of outworn clothing they gowned the Corn Maiden, and Ariella crowned the doll with her own wreath.

Then they passed the Corn Maiden to the rest, who bore her in triumph to the groaning trestle-tables arranged in front of the Manor, as the last rays of the sun gilded the tops of the trees.

They set the Corn Maiden in the place of honor above the feast as men lit the great torches of pitch and straw that had been set about the tables, and the folk of the Manor took places on the seats of log that had been set around the makeshift tables.

An ox had been roasted whole for this feast, nor was that all; the kitchen staff had outdone themselves, with every other tasty dish that could be imagined. There was enough to stuff everyone to capacity and still have leftovers to share out.

Ariella's only regret was that Merod could not be here; she imagined how his eyes would sparkle at the fun and how he would toss his head and perhaps even join in the dancing.

The air hummed with laughter and talk, the torchlight shone on happy faces, and once the edge was off her hunger, Ariella nibbled and watched, taking it all in.

She glanced to the side to see how Lady Magda fared. Even that Lady had lost some of her haughty reserve, unbending enough to smile and joke with the Abbot at her other side.

The small army of Manor-folk decimated the piles of food. As the stars came out and circled overhead, the ox was reduced to a skeleton, the mounds of vegetables melted away like snow in the spring, the bread developed gaping holes and the pies and cakes eroded to pitiful remnants of their former glorious selves. Now it was time for the traditional toasts, and Lord Kaelin stood up, tankard in hand, to begin them.

Something icy, foreboding and grim seized Ariella's heart, and she swiftly turned her gaze from the expectant faces below her to her father's countenance.

As that cold hand gripped her soul and froze her where she sat, she saw, as if in a nightmare, her father open his lips—try to speak—

—a puzzled look came into his eyes—he blinked in shock and surprise—

—and toppled over, crashing into the table before him.

Ariella screamed and leapt for him, arms outstretched as her chair fell over backwards.

Pandemonium. Men shouted, women screamed or

wailed, children began crying. Some rushed for the high table, some to get water, some shouted confused instructions. Ariella frantically turned her father over, crying out his name—but the icy hand that held her heart was the chill and unforgiving hand of death, and she knew he could no longer hear her.

Someone pulled her away, more people held her, keeping her from her father's side. She screamed and wept, fighting them, trying to get back to his side, thinking surely there must be something she could do, yet knowing there was nothing to be done.

Then the moment of shock passed and the grief came, and her legs gave out beneath her. Hands held her up, the Abbot's, the steward's; there was nothing in her heart and mind but loss, nothing in her soul but grief, nothing in her world but tears. She collapsed, her throat closing, her body knotted about itself, her hands reaching for something she could never grasp. Animal moans of grief spilled from her, and she shook as though with fever.

They led her away, knotted and tangled in her terrible grief, unable to see, to think, to feel anything now but a vast and lonely emptiness.

They took her to her room, coaxed her to drink something—something bitter, but not so bitter as the tears that burned her eyes and scorched her cheeks.

She fell from tears into darkness and knew nothing more for a day and a night.

The next days passed as in a nightmare from which there was no waking. Ariella wept until her eyes were sore and swollen, and still there were tears left over. The Abbot murmured words meant to comfort that she did not hear, Lady Magda plied her with platitudes she ignored. She tried to go to the forest more than once, but those watching her prevented her, and she didn't have the strength to fight them. Finally the Abbot brought the Infirmarian, and there was more of the bitter drink, and her days faded into a haze of drug and tears.

She walked through a dim world of shadows and sorrow. On a day gone chill and gray, Lord Kaelin was buried. Overnight, it seemed, all the light and joy had gone out of the universe, the trees turned to leafless skeletons, the sky to endless slate-colored clouds, and the wind bit with teeth of ice. People came and went, strangers she didn't know. They sat her down in her father's study, then discussed her fate as if she wasn't there.

"She fades more with every day," Lady Magda whispered to her maid on the morning of yet another dreary day, as both of them cast furtive glances out of the corners of their eyes to where Ariella sat, listlessly, in the window-seat.

"Things will change when *he* comes," the pert maid

replied with a knowing wink. Ariella rubbed her eyes and wondered dimly who "he" was. There had been a great deal of talk about some man she had never heard of. The Abbot had explained it to her, they said. Something about Swan Manor . . . that as a woman she could not inherit, but that . . . something . . . had been arranged with her nearest male relative, a cousin. She licked her lips and stared out the window at the leafless trees tossing their skeletal branches in the wind, clawing the sky with bone-thin fingers. She only hoped that her cousin, whoever he was, would make these people leave her in peace. She only wanted to mourn and to see Merod. She longed for Merod with a need that was near to starvation. Merod would know what to say, how to help her ease her loss, how to make her see beyond all this sorrow.

"Here, child, let me tidy you," Lady Magda was saying, and Ariella let herself be drawn from the window-seat, let them comb and braid her hair, put it in a silver net, and arrange a fine veil over it. Just as they finished primping her as if she was a giant doll, one of the servants appeared in the door of her room.

"He's here, Lady Magda!" the girl said excitedly. "He's waiting in the great hall!"

Still fussing with the veil, Lady Magda drew Ariella to her feet and pulled her along by the hand. "Come, child, it's time to meet your cousin. Let's have no more sulks, but only smiles."

Smiles? What did she have to smile about? But Magda wouldn't hear a word she said, so she didn't even try to contradict the old biddy; she simply let herself be drawn along in Magda's bustling wake to the great hall, where candles flickered uneasily in the drafts, and the room seemed suddenly too small to contain all the huge and armored men who crowded into it. Strange, dark faces beneath coifs of chain turned to stare at them as they entered at the door.

"Here she is!" Magda sang out. "Here's your little maid, Lord Lyon!"

Before Ariella could wonder who Lord Lyon was, the sea of tall, grimly dark men parted, and a single golden figure strode out of their midst.

He alone of all of them was bare-headed, and his hair was as brilliantly sun-hued as the grain at harvest. His chainmail armor had been washed with gold, and it glittered in the candlelight. Over it he wore a surcoat of brilliant scarlet, with a seated lion embroidered proudly on the front. He was taller by half a head than the men around him, with piercing black eyes, a jutting chin, and a firm mouth, which just now was smiling as he held out both hands towards her.

"Lady Ariella! We meet at long last!" he boomed in an overwhelmingly loud and deep voice as he seized both her hands in his, hands which engulfed hers completely. "They told me you were the image of your blessed

71

mother, and they spoke truth! Truly the Wild Swan of Swan Manor is the loveliest maiden in all the world!"

Everything about him was—much too large, too overpowering. Ariella stared at him in confusion, trying to make some sense out of what he said. He bent to kiss her hands and she looked down at the top of his head with its sun-gold curls cascading down the back of his neck, wanting to pull her hands away from his proprietary, too-firm grip and not daring to. He looked up, and caught her gazing at him; she glanced away in confusion, feeling heat mount in her cheeks as he straightened again, towering above her.

"Ah, shy, sweeting? No matter. A little shyness is a proper thing in a maiden." He turned his head and looked past her at Lady Magda. "I have no cause to regret our fathers' pact, cousin Magda. Your lady is all the prize that rumor claimed her to be. I shall be glad and proud to be the man who tamed the Wild Swan."

Pact? Prize? Ariella finally reclaimed her hands and twisted them together as she tried to make something of the perplexing words. What pact? Was there—she tried to recall—something that the Abbot had said?

The man was still speaking, although Ariella had lost the first few words. ". . . be on our way," he said to Lady Magda. "Immediately. We have much to do."

"Oh, surely you'll stay a fortnight at least," Lady Magda protested. "The child has only just buried her poor father! And surely you'll wish to look over the Manor!"

There was steel beneath the man's voice, and his brows creased together in a faint frown. "I fear that is hardly possible," he replied. "I have my own lands to see to, after all, and I must assemble a gathering of guests and witnesses before the snow flies to make our pact binding. My steward will take care of everything necessary here— you, of course, will remain as chatelaine to see to the domestic affairs. I trust that the Lady's gear is packed and ready to be taken?"

"Well, y-y-yes," Lady Magda stammered. A single wave of his hand dismissed any other words she might say. "Then get your Lady's cloak, have her litter prepared, and we will be off!" he said imperiously. "My steward will take charge here for me, and he will take the room that was Lady Ariella's. Obey his orders as you would mine, for he will be reporting directly to me. We have far to travel before night comes upon us!"

Pact? Ariella thought with growing dismay. *Steward?* She looked about her for help, but there was no one she knew nearby. She was completely surrounded by tall, dark-visaged men in armor whose slate-gray surcoats swallowed up the light of the room. Before she knew what she was about, Lord Lyon had swept her cloak about her shoulders and fastened it at her chin, then gathered her up in one muscular arm and half-carried her out of the great hall, through the front door, and into the cold wind outside.

The horse-litter that Lady Magda used stood ready just outside the door, two sturdy mules bearing its weight, and Lord Lyon picked up Ariella as easily as a baby chick and deposited her inside, shutting the curtains on her protests. Tangled in her skirts and cloak, still dizzy with the Infirmier's bitter potion, she tried to disentangle herself in the chill darkness of the horse-litter, but before she could even get one foot free, the mules moved forward with a lurch that sent her crashing into the cushions. "Wait!" she called, struggling with cloak, furs, and cushions. "What does all of this mean? I don't want to leave! Stop!"

But no one paid her any attention—in fact, she wasn't certain anyone heard her, and soon the mules were moving at a pace that sent the litter swaying and jostling, so that she could hardly get a full breath.

She had never traveled by litter, and between her drug-hazed mind and the lurching of the litter, it was all she could do to keep herself from being knocked senseless, much less escape from the stuffy, cold, cramped little box. Where was she going? Where was this man taking her? And most important of all, *why?*

Her head had cleared a little, but in place of the dazed and dizzy feeling, a headache had begun just behind her eyes. It was quite dark when the mules finally stopped moving, firelight flickered in the gap between the curtains, and a hand clad in a thick leather gauntlet shoved the curtains aside. "We've made camp, my Lady," said a brusque and unfamiliar male voice. "I fear that a tent is the best we can offer you."

She peeked out of the litter cautiously as the man extended a hand to help her down out of it. They were in the midst of an unfamiliar wilderness of huge pine trees that moaned and sighed in the cold wind, swaying back and forth as if they were about to pull up their roots and dance. The litter had halted beside a roaring fire, with a small tent on the opposite side. Behind her, she heard the sounds of horses stamping and chewing; before her, men laid out bedrolls beside the fire on the bare ground, while one skewered rabbits on a spit, preparing to prop them over the flames. She tried not to look, swallowing hard.

Lord Lyon strode out of the shadows and brushed aside his henchman's hand, putting both hands on her waist and lifting her down out of the litter. "A rough welcome, my Lady, but you'll have a better at Lyon Castle," he proclaimed as if to a multitude, gesturing at the fire and the tent. "I am sorry that your woman wasn't fit for such a harsh journey, but you'll have maids a-plenty waiting for you at home, and I'm sure you can fend for yourself for a few days."

"Home?" she managed. "I was home! Why am I here? Where are you taking me?"

He looked down at her with a patronizing smile. "You are coming with me, sweeting. Surely your Abbot explained it all to you, did he not?"

She put a hand to her aching forehead and blinked, trying to think through the growing pain and the sick feeling in her stomach. "I—I'm not sure. They gave me something to drink—things were very confused. I remember—the Abbot did talk to me, but I can't recall what he said—"

"And in your grief, you were not thinking of anything else, of course," he said soothingly, still with that superior smile. "Well, it is simple, Lady Ariella. Your father held Swan Manor without a son to inherit from him. As a woman, you cannot inherit any property. You have your dower-portion, of course, but no property. Had you wedded while your father was still alive, Swan Manor would

have gone to your first-born son, with your husband holding it in trust for him, but since you were still a maid—"
He shrugged. "As your nearest male kin, I was to inherit
the Manor if your father died before you were wed, but
neither your father nor mine cared to think of you going
to the charity of the Church or making some hasty and
imprudent alliance in that case, so they made a pact that
if you had not found a husband by the time your father
died, and I had not found a wife, then I would wed you,
thus keeping Swan Manor in your bloodline and saving
you from being displaced. It was all arranged a very long
time ago, and your father probably never wanted you to
bother your pretty head about it."

Simple? *Simple?* She stared at him, her head and heart
pounding together, too utterly appalled and shocked to
say a single word.

"I must admit that I was quite well pleased to find my
bride to be so comely," he continued with an expression

she could only think of as a smug smirk. "I find myself with a very fine bargain, and I am sure you are hardly displeased with the sight of your intended husband!" His grin widened and he puffed out his chest a bit, and some of his men laughed out loud. "As to where we are going, we travel to my own estate, where we will be properly wedded in the sight of witnesses and kindred." His expression turned a touch threatening. "I will have this done properly. I would not have it rumored that your hand and land should have gone elsewhere, that our kinship is too close for matrimony, or that our union is no true marriage. There will be no reason to protest that this union is invalid."

By this time he had led her, step by step, to the door of the tent. Now he pulled the flap aside and held it open for her. "And now I will leave you to your well-guarded and well-deserved rest, my Lady. I am sure so delicate a maid as you must be fatigued by the journey. One of my men will bring you something to eat, and you may sleep when you will, knowing that we guard you as we would any precious object."

A slight nudge sent her stumbling into the tent, and he dropped the flap shut behind her, leaving her in a canvas shelter illuminated only by the firelight filtering through the fabric. With a little moan of pain and incredulity, she sank down on the pile of bedding at her feet, drained of strength and will.

She woke in the morning, certain it had all been a terrible nightmare, only to find that the nightmare had not passed with the coming of daylight. She opened her eyes to find herself staring at a canvas roof, head aching, bundled in blankets that smelled of smoke and horses. Around the tent outside, men tramped about, making thumping and clattering noises; she heard shouting, harnesses jingling, and horses stamping and neighing. Her head throbbed abominably, but her mind was clearer now.

Too clear, perhaps, for she could see no way to escape from this trap. She did not know where she was, she could hardly run off on foot into a strange forest with no weapons and no provisions. It was unlikely that with so many alert men about, she would be able to steal a horse and escape, and even if she could, where would she go? She didn't even know what direction to travel to return to Swan Manor, and if she did find her way home, Lord Lyon would only come to take her again. She could run off to the forest and hope that she could elude him there—but she shrank from the idea of all those armored men with their iron and steel rampaging about near her Faerie friends.

Before her thoughts went any further, the tent-flap was pulled aside and Lord Lyon shoved a round of cold bread and a cold rabbit-quarter at her without any kind of greeting or warning. She took it reflexively and stared at him with stinging eyes.

"Break your fast, Lady Ariella, and let us be up and away!" he said so loudly that she winced. "We have far to go, and the sooner we are upon the journey, the sooner we will reach home!"

"Aye, soonest wedded and soonest bedded," called one of his men, and another guffawed as Ariella held the hastily proffered food with one hand, stood up, and shook herself free of the bedclothes. She had gone to sleep fully dressed, so there was little for her to do to "make ready"—but no sooner had she stood free of the blankets than one of the men bustled into the tent and bundled up her erstwhile sleeping-place, carrying it off to stow in a pack somewhere. She clutched the bread and meat, trying not to cry, wondering what to do next, and the tent began to teeter above her as other men pulled up its stakes. She hastily got out of the way, only to find herself seized by the waist and swinging through the air as Lord Lyon hoisted her into her litter again.

"You'll find better provisioning here today, my Lady," he said as he closed the curtains on her. "We won't be stopping till nightfall, so make yourself free of it when you've a mind to refresh yourself."

She was still clutching the bread and cold meat; he had not even given her the chance to take or refuse the crude breakfast. In the gloom of the horse-litter, in the farther corner she made out a pale bundle among the furs and traveling rugs. As the mules started forward with a jerk, she pulled it toward her.

She wrestled the knots holding it shut with chilled fingers while the litter swayed and jounced between the two mules. The white cloth finally parted beneath her numb hands and fell open, and by touch and scent she recognized the vague shapes as cheese, apples, more bread, and a leather bottle, carefully stoppered shut. She levered the stopper out and sniffed cautiously; it held wine, rather than the herb tea or water that she would have preferred. She didn't think her aching head would be well-served by drinking it.

For that matter, her stomach wasn't particularly enamored of the greasy, half-burnt meat, the strong cheese, or the stale bread. As her head continued to pound, she huddled miserably into the furs and wondered what would become of her.

Slow tears slipped down her cheeks and dropped onto the fur. She choked down a sob, which lodged in her throat and remained there, a cold ball of ice that resisted swallowing. Never had she felt so alone, so helpless, and so deserted. How could her Papa have left her to this?

She jumped, holding in a gasp, as the sound of voices just behind her startled her.

"Have you seen anything?" That was Lord Lyon's

booming voice, and she shrank instinctively away from the sound.

"Wolf sign, nothing more. No sign of Faerie—"

"Quiet, you fool!" Lord Lyon snapped. "Don't you know better than to speak of them out loud?" His horse snorted and the harness jingled. "You're sure you haven't seen anything?"

"Absolutely sure." The man laughed. "Not that they would come anywhere near this much iron and steel. Why are you so concerned? You've never fretted about meeting them on the road before."

"There are rumors—" Lord Lyon growled. "Rumors my young bride has had doings with them, and she's got a fey look about her to back those rumors. She's comely enough for them to want her, and I've heard they don't look kindly on those who make a claim on maidens they've taken an interest in. I'm not minded to risk the loss of so fine a manor and lands when I'm so close to taking possession of them, and I've no intention of finding myself in some magical battle just because one of them wants her back."

The other man laughed again. "Well, you'll have plenty of iron, steel, and holy men between you and their wiles once we're back at Lyon Castle. And besides all that protection, you'll have all of your men alert and standing between as well. Nothing will get in— or out."

"Meaning?" Lord Lyon asked a trifle suspiciously.

"Meaning that if they try to call her outside your protection—or she takes a notion to try to run—we'll be there to make certain she won't get far." The man's matter-of-fact tone sent cold threads of fear down Ariella's back. "Then it'll be up to you to make her see reason—or get her with child so she'll have other things to think of, and they'll lose interest in her."

Lord Lyon snorted, and Ariella shook at the thought that he might decide to anticipate the marriage vows, given that bit of advice. "That'll happen as soon as the blessing's pronounced," he replied arrogantly. Then, before she could overhear anything else, someone shouted up ahead and their horses trotted off.

Her head spun with disconnected images and fears, making her feel sick with anxiety. All she could do was cling with both hands to the edge of her cloak and weep silently into the darkness.

But by the time they stopped for the night, she had found a touch of courage somewhere. Perhaps it had come from that overheard conversation—for if Lord Lyon was afraid that her Faerie friends were following, well, perhaps they were! She made up her mind that she would try to escape and take her chances in the forest.

After all, I've nothing to fear from the animals! she reminded herself. *Only from humans.*

So when Lord Lyon lifted her out of the litter into the

night-shrouded camp, she clutched the bundle of un-eaten provisions to her. Those, she would certainly need!

Silent, she walked obediently behind him. Silent, she entered the tent. Silent still, crouching on her bed of furs and blankets, she waited for the noise and voices outside the tent walls to die out.

She was cold and stiff by the time the last voices died and the flickering firelight lending false warmth to the tent walls faded somewhat. Then, when everything was quiet and even the crackle of the fire had turned to the hiss of coals, she moved.

But she did not raise the flap in the front of the tent. Instead, working stealthily, she worked at the canvas at the back, until she pried up two of the stakes holding it to the cold ground, giving her enough of a gap to squeeze out.

She raised the canvas—pushed her bundle of provisions out and followed it on hands and knees—

And found herself nose-to-toe with a pair of large, black boots.

She looked up; looking down at her was one of the coldest pair of eyes in one of the stoniest faces she had ever seen.

The man said nothing; he only continued to stare down at her. Her mouth went dry as dust, and still he did not move. Finally, after a long, long time, she pulled her head back into the tent, leaving her bundle of food behind. After another minute or two, someone hammered the stakes she had pulled up back into the ground with heavy, angry blows.

She waited, sleepless, for the rest of the night, fearing punishment, anger, she knew not what. Dawn crawled into the camp, gray and dingy; the noise of men rousing began.

Then, finally, the tent-flap jerked open, seized by a rough hand, and Lord Lyon stood looking down at her. She started to shiver, teeth chattering in her fear.

He held out a leather tankard. She stared at it.

"I think," he said, in a false, warm voice, "That you are in need for your physik, my Lady." He thrust the tankard at her.

"Drink," he ordered in a suddenly changed voice, a voice that warned that if she did not drink, the brew would be poured down her unwilling throat.

With nerveless, shaking hands, half spilling the potion, she drank, and she recognized the bitter taste. Lord Lyon took back the empty tankard as she dropped it. A sudden dizziness overwhelmed her.

Then her eyes closed of themselves; she felt him lift her up and carry her, and she knew nothing more until nightfall.

She tried to refuse to drink again, but she was given no choice. After four dreadful days and nights, marked only by drugged haze, chill, sick fear, grief, and a growing desperation, she thought there would be no end to the horrible journey. Then on the fifth morning, she was not drugged—as the morning passed, then midday, the last of the drug wore off, and she regained her wits somewhat. Finally the mules stopped, and for the first time it was in the middle of the day. She remained huddled in the litter, afraid to look out, but gnawed with an anxious need to know what was happening.

The decision on what to do was taken out of her hands. That now-familiar leather gauntlet shoved the curtains aside, and Lord Lyon's voice rang out with hearty cheer that she knew now was all too false.

"Come out and look upon your new home, sweeting! We are here at last!"

He pulled her from the litter without giving her a chance to move her own stiff limbs, then set her down on the roadway with a smacking kiss on her forehead.

"There you are, my Lady!" he crowed, waving his hand with proprietary pride. "Lyon Castle! I'll wager you've never seen its like before!"

That much was certainly the truth. Her cozy and welcoming home was nothing like this.

Lyon Castle was as grim and imposing as the tall men that guarded it, a huge pile of stone and iron that loomed gray and cheerless against the overcast sky. Armed men patrolled the top of the crenellated wall surrounding it, and more armed men stood watch on top of towers at each corner of the walls. No welcoming lights gleamed at the windows, because there were no windows, only mere defensive slits in the thick rock walls. A formidable portcullis, just now drawn up, defended the entrance with fangs of blackened iron. It made the entrance look exactly like the open maw of a terrible monster. At her feet a moat full of dark, chill water encircled the castle and its grounds, with the drawbridge now down and extending from the road where she stood to the entrance. There was no crowd of welcomers standing on the other side of the bridge, only another pair of dour, armored guards in slate-gray surcoats, one on either side of the entranceway.

If her legs had been steadier, she would have turned and run at that moment. But her knees trembled and threatened to give way under her, and Lord Lyon's firm grip on her arm seemed impossible to dislodge. He marched cheerfully towards the fangs of his portcullis, drawing her with him, and his men marched behind, their spurs ringing with each step.

Once inside the entrance, she heard the portcullis groan as it was lowered into place behind her, chains clanking and clattering until it dropped into position with a final, echoing thud.

The entrance was a long, dark tunnel beneath the walls, lit by a pair of smoking torches. It ended in a bare little courtyard open to the ashen sky, at a huge wooden double door with massive iron hinges, half of which swung open as they approached. More guards waited inside, and Lord Lyon urged her onwards as she felt the walls closing in around her like a trap.

The entryway, dark and ill-lit by more torches, was nearly as cold as the road outside. Huge chairs of dark wood, elaborately carved and uncompromisingly uncomfortable, stood against the wall, which was not even softened by so much as a single tapestry. A staircase descended to this stone-walled entryway, and three women, the first Ariella had seen in four days, moved quietly down it towards them.

The woman in the lead was older than Ariella, though not as old as Lady Magda; sleek and sensual, black of hair and gray of eye, with a perfectly sculpted face that showed not a trace of emotion. Gowned in a velvet of deep blue, bound around with a silver-chain chatelaine belt, with a silver crucifix at her neck and a thin silver band binding her hair, Ariella knew she must be a woman of rank—or at least, importance. The two younger girls behind her, fresh-faced, brown-cheeked maids with brown hair, wearing simple chemises and woolen smocks, were clearly servants.

"Lady Katherine! I put my bride gratefully into your hands!" Lord Lyon called out without bothering to hide his relief. "Lady Katherine, this is the Lady Ariella, my distant cousin. Ariella, this is Lady Katherine, my chatelaine, and stepdaughter to my father's oldest and nearest ally, Count Andrew of Loderdale."

Neither of the names meant anything to Ariella. As Lord Lyon stalked off down a hallway, leaving Ariella standing there alone, Lady Katherine looked her up and down without losing a whit of her cool composure.

"Well," Lady Katherine said, her voice just as unemotional as her expression, "you must be chilled and weary, Ariella. Let me show you to your chamber."

That was the last thing that Ariella wanted, but it would do her no good to protest at this point. She simply let Lady Katherine lead the way back up the stairs, trailed by the two maids, who whispered to each other behind her back.

Drafts gusted up the staircase behind them, making the torches flare and smoke in their sconces, as they wound their way up and up the spiral stone stair until Ariella was afraid she would not be able to go another step. Then, just when she was ready to drop, Lady Katherine paused at a landing before a small wooden door and opened it without a word, leaving Ariella to follow her inside. A guard stood at that landing, a guard with the same cold, dead eyes as the one that had caught her trying to escape.

Ariella was afraid at this point that "her chamber" was going to be as cold and cheerless as every other place in this castle. But although the rooms beyond were stone-walled and stone-floored like the rest, here at least there was light and warmth, and some effort had been made to cut off the drafts and create some comfort.

Panels of thin-sliced horn covered the slit-windows, allowing some light to come in from outside. Instead of smoking torches, fine wax candles as thick as her wrist provided plenty of clear illumination. Tapestries covered the walls, and furs and rugs placed over a layer of rushes strewn with lavender softened and warmed the floors. A fine fire burned on the hearths in both the outer and inner rooms, and charcoal braziers added their warmth from each corner. The outer room was furnished with a desk, several chairs, and an embroidery frame; the inner held a canopied and curtained bed. Several chests waited in the inner room as well, one of them open, and Ariella caught a glimpse of a familiar dress trailing over the side.

"This will be your set of chambers, Ariella," the chatelaine said. "You won't be expected to share Lord Lyon's rooms, of course; he has men coming and going at all hours of the day and night, and you would be constantly disturbed. He will join you here, at the proper times." Lady Katherine kept her eyes hooded, but Ariella caught a flash of satisfaction when Ariella winced at the mention of Lord Lyon "joining" her. "The maids and I will finish unpacking your possessions and I have sent for some dinner for you. Why don't you warm yourself at the fire while you wait for it?"

Ariella mutely did as she was told, allowing one maid to take her cloak before dropping down into the chair nearest the fire. She knew that she looked much the worse for wear, rumpled and tired, pale and travel-stained, but she didn't care; she was just too exhausted. At least she was somewhere warm and no longer in that cursed horse-litter.

Food came and was presented to her; she ate part of it without tasting it. Lady Katherine sailed out with a tiny smile on her lips; one maid followed the chatelaine with the tray of half-eaten food, the other remained behind. She took Ariella into the inner room, and helped her out of her crumpled, dirty gown and into a night-dress warmed before the fire. The maid sat her down on a stool in front of the hearth, combed out and braided her hair and put her to bed, closing the curtains around her. Ariella heard her footsteps retreating, heard the door open and close, and she was finally alone.

But as tired as she was, she was not at all sleepy; she was too tense and unhappy for that. The warmth and food finally eased the ache in her head and the knot in her stomach, but nothing could help the pain in her heart or the feeling of helpless entrapment.

She clenched her hands together and tried to think of something she could do—there must be some way that she could escape from here!

The only way in or out of these two rooms was the

stair—guarded at her door, with probably another guard at the bottom of the staircase. Then there were more guards at the front door, and at the portcullis. How could she ever get past them? *Could I disguise myself somehow?* Where would she get a disguise, though? This wasn't Swan Manor, where she knew every storage-place and every closet and had the keys to all of them. Lady Katherine was the one in charge here, and Ariella didn't think that Lady Katherine was going to prove to be any kind of an ally.

Could I make a disguise? That seemed a little more likely—she shouldn't have too much difficulty getting Lady Katherine to give her lengths of the common fabrics that the serving-maids wore. *I could say I wanted to sew for the poor. I don't think that would make anyone suspicious.* But making a disguise would take time and would have to be done in secret—it might be months before she had anything usable.

But it's going to take me months to find out where I am, and figure out where I can go if I do get away. . . . Taking sanctuary at a convent was possible, but risky; if the Sisters found out who and what she was, they'd probably turn her back over to her husband. She wanted to go home, but Lady Magda would be of no help. Dare she seek help from the serfs? Could she ask help of the Faerie? After all, she had been helping them—but would they dare the threat of Lord Lyon's iron swords?

Unprovisioned, she couldn't leave until spring or she'd die in the wilderness or along the road.

By then, what would have happened? She shuddered as she recalled Lord Lyon's crude boast that he would have her with child as soon as the blessing had been pronounced. If she could get her hands on her simples, there were ways to prevent conception—she wasn't supposed to know them, but she did. But would Lord Lyon—or Lady Katherine—know those ways, too, and be guarding against them?

Women died in childbirth all the time. Her own mother had died in childbirth. Lord Lyon didn't need her, once he'd wed her and had a son ... and Lady Katherine did not look like the kind of woman who was inclined to take second place to anyone.

I have to get away! If she'd been a bird, she'd have beaten her wings bloody against the bars of this, her cage. Her hands pulled at the neck of her bedgown as her throat tightened and it seemed harder to breathe.

It felt as if she had been lying in the stuffy darkness for hours, as if she would lie here forever. Then somehow she crossed from waking into sleep, into restless nightmares in which she tried endlessly to escape from a forest of trees that turned into iron-clad guards who shouted and grabbed at her as she passed them.

Then it was morning and one of the maidservants pulled the bed-curtains wide, startling her into wakefulness.

"You'll be wanting a bath, my Lady, after you break your fast," the maid said cheerfully. "My Lord Lyon will be entertaining his guests without you, so we'll have all day to ready you before your wedding tomorrow. We'll fit your gown to you and make sure you go to the altar shining like a star." She beamed at Ariella. "Lord Lyon is a fine figure of a man, and you will want to look your loveliest for him."

No, I won't! she wanted to scream, but she could only nod numbly.

With her stomach in knots again, it was just as well that they didn't give her much time to eat. The maid brought porridge on a tray, and new milk. She managed to drink the milk and forced a few bites down her throat, then set the tray aside. Before she'd even gotten out of bed, two male servants hauled a huge tub into the first room and set it up before the fire. Right after the tub came a parade of maids with buckets of hot water, a mountain of towels, screens to set up around the tub to hide her from view of the door, soaps, perfumes, and scented oils.

Once again she was treated like a giant doll; two maids stripped her to the skin and unbraided her hair. They assisted her into the tub and wouldn't even let her wash herself; they scrubbed every bit of her as if they suspected she'd never had a thorough bath before, rinsed her with more clean water, then washed her hair three times with three different concoctions, and rinsed it with rose-water. They rubbed her with scented oils, wrapped her in towels, and sat her down beside the fire while three of them combed her hair with ivory combs until it was dry.

By now, the morning was completely gone. They brought her more food, which she pretended to eat while they cleared away the bath-things. As soon as the room was clear, they whisked the food away, then braided up her hair and wound it around her head and assisted her into a thin, clinging silk slip of a chemise.

Now came the dressmakers, bearing the wedding finery, and she shrank inside herself when she saw it. But there was no hope for her; she was surrounded by maidservants and seamstresses, with Lady Katherine to oversee them all, and she didn't have a prayer of escaping from them.

It was a sumptuous gown, but of an antique style, and she suspected it had been the Lyon wedding gown for several generations, carefully preserved and fitted to each new Lyon bride, setting the Lyon stamp on her before the vows were even spoken.

Up onto a stool she went, and the fittings began. First the underdress, a fall of ivory samite with closely fitted sleeves, coming down to points on the backs of each hand, and laced tight about the body. It had a modest train and very little trim, just gold embroidery on the hems and at the neck. But it had to fit perfectly, without a wrinkle, and the seamstresses seemed determined that nothing less than perfection would do. Eventually, Lady Katherine gave a reluctant nod, and the undergown was deemed suitable.

When they were finally satisfied with the underdress, it was time for the gown. This was a heavy silk damask of scarlet, with huge, trailing open sleeves lined and trimmed in ermine, a train longer than she was tall, embroidered all over with sitting lions in gold. This, too, must fit closely to the body, with never a wrinkle or a pucker. It was terribly heavy, and the weight of the train alone was enough to make her shoulders ache. The seamstresses kept fussing around her, taking tiny, invisible tucks and stitches, never satisfied even when she was unable to see anything amiss.

When they finally stood away from her and their frowns turned to smiles, she sighed, thinking that they were done. But they weren't.

Next to be fitted to her was a set of jewels; a heavy belt

made of gold lions' heads with ruby eyes, a matching necklace, and matching armbands that clasped about her upper arms, just where the huge sleeves started to bell out. Then came a veil of the same ivory samite as the undergown, also embroidered with gold around the hem and held in place with a circlet of gold studded with tiny rubies. All these required more fussing and fitting until her head throbbed and her vision blurred.

At long last, seamstresses, jewelers, and Lady Katherine all declared themselves satisfied. Once again Ariella was stripped to the skin, the wedding finery arrayed on stands until the morrow, and Ariella was allowed to put on a simple woolen gown and come down off the stool.

But not to rest—no, now came a dozen pairs of silken hose to try on, then shoemakers, who took tracings of her feet and cut soles then and there, which they sewed to the embroidered tops of red damask slippers to match the gown. They had to make a total of a half dozen shoes and fit them to her feet before Lady Katherine judged two of the shoes suitable and permitted them to be placed with the gown.

Lady Katherine left without having said a word directly to her all afternoon. Her captors allowed her to have a little rest; supper arrived, though all Ariella could really eat was the soup and some bread.

She had hardly finished that when the maidservants returned carrying a vast array of cosmetic jars. They stripped her to the skin again, directed her to lie down on a rug in front of the fire, and went to work, rubbing creams and unguents into her skin, unbraiding her hair again and combing perfumes through it. With one maid for each hand and one for each foot, her nails were filed to perfect ovals and buffed until they achieved a pearl-like gloss; every trace of a callus had been removed, and her skin was as soft as a rose-petal.

All this would have been very pleasant if she hadn't

felt exactly like a pagan sacrifice being prepared for the knife.

While the maids worked, they chattered in high, breathy voices, like the twittering of little birds. Ariella would rather they'd been silent, for all they could talk about was the wedding celebration of the morrow and the feast still going on somewhere below.

"There's a fountain of silver that will be pouring wine for everyone," sighed one. "I watched them setting it up—"

"Well, I've seen the cages of bears for baiting, and you should have heard them roar!" The girl shivered pleasurably. "They are monstrously fierce, and they'll make a fine showing against the dogs!"

"Pooh, who cares for such things when there will be dancing?" asked a third, industriously polishing the nails of Ariella's right hand. "I've heard the hired minstrels, and they are wonderful!"

"Well, I've got a surprise for you all, for I was at the feast tonight, and there's a magician come! Lord Lyon agreed to let him work some splendid magics at the wedding ceremony itself!" crowed the one at Ariella's left hand in triumph.

"What?" "A magician?" "But Lord Lyon doesn't care for magicians—" All the rest spoke at once, and the knowing one waved them to silence.

"He will, I tell you, for I was there!" she declared. "He asked to be admitted to the feast and presented himself to Lord Lyon—and oh! I swear to you that I have never seen a handsomer man except the Lord himself! Hair as long as my arm and so black! Face like a pagan god, with such green eyes! Dressed all in black velvet he was, too; it was clear to see that he was not only a magician, but a man of noble birth." She sighed, and the others twittered to each other. "He made his compliments to the Lord, said he was from some outlandish foreign land, and begged that he might have the honor of performing magic for the wedding to make it the talk of the land. Lord Lyon was suspicious, but the fellow kissed a cross and held a sword, so he wasn't one of—*them*—so it was all right. Lord Lyon asked what he planned to do, and the man said that he would give the Lord a smaller entertainment right then!"

"Well?" "Then what?"

The maid laughed. "Oh, I wish you had seen it! First he made a fog rise up in the middle of the floor, then a tree grew up through the fog, all bare branches, but shining like gold. Then the branches suddenly burst out in emerald leaves and rosy flowers, then the flowers turned to scarlet fruit, then the fruit burst open to release a flock of birds all in yellow and red and green that flew up to the ceiling and disappeared! Then the leaves on the tree turned red and gold and fell to the floor, and the branches of the tree shot fountains of fire, and then the whole thing vanished into thin air!"

Ariella thought with an aching heart of the beautiful visions that Merod had conjured, and wondered how anything so tawdry as the girl had described could compare to the glimpse she'd had of the Great Ones dancing. Some southern mountebank, likely, with cheap illusions that passed for real magic among those who had never seen the genuine article.

The maids, however, were more than impressed with their fellow servant's description and voiced their envy while speculating on what the foreign magician might produce on the morrow. One girl voted for a troop of knights on winged horses to escort the bride and groom, one for a forest of silver and gold trees with fiery birds singing wedding songs, and one for fountains of sparks and fire, and great fiery bursts of sky-illuminations, with an invisible band of musicians playing in accompaniment.

When they had finished turning Ariella into a soft, primped, perfumed and polished creature she hardly recognized, they assisted her into a fine nightgown, gave her a hot, sweet posset to drink, and put her to bed. There must have been something akin to the Abbot's potion in the drink, for she fell asleep before they finished closing the curtains around her.

The maids woke her at daybreak, singing as they brought the wedding dress to her. It might just as well have been a shroud, for she felt no joy in seeing it, only despair and a wild wish to rend it to pieces and escape.

But there was no escape, and the maids encased her in the heavy, entrapping folds of the dress, then smothered her in the veil, with her hair loose and unbound beneath it. They weighed her down with chains and fetters in the form of jewelry and exclaimed how lovely she was. Then they led her down to meet her doom.

At the foot of the stairs, Lord Lyon waited with a troop

of his guards, all garbed for the occasion in splendid red surcoats over their mail like the one the Lord himself had worn the day he came for her. He, for once, was not in armor; he wore a scarlet damask robe that matched her gown, and he took her hand with a smile so feral and hungry that she shrank inside the heavy gown, feeling her heart contract to a hard, cold knot.

He said nothing but simply led her along yet another torchlit hall to another door. This one led to a stone-paved courtyard filled with people in festive array, and a low platform on the opposite side held a portable altar and a man in the robes of a priest.

But a handsome, striking man standing immediately before them was not in the bright peacock colors of the rest of the guests. Instead, he was clothed from head to foot in black velvet, even to boots and gloves of the same material. He bowed when Lord Lyon appeared, and stepped forward, holding out his hands.

"For you, my Lord, to place your seal upon your bride," the man said in a melodious tenor as he placed a massive gold ring in the shape of a lion with ruby eyes in the Lord's hand. "Remembering that some things must be grasped and held against all odds."

Lord Lyon exclaimed with pleasure, for the ring was of such fine workmanship that every hair in the lion's mane had been perfectly formed, and the rubies flashed with far more fire than the ones Ariella wore. But the beauty of the ring gave Ariella no pleasure, only a further sinking of her heart.

But the man had turned to her, and had taken her free hand, placing something into it and clasping her fingers around it. "For you, Wild Swan," he said—and there was something about his voice, and something in his emerald-green eyes, that seemed strangely and tantalizingly familiar. "Remembering that some things are meant to be shared."

He dropped her hand; whatever he had put in it was round, cold and hard—but it didn't feel like a ring. She relaxed her fingers a little, just as he stepped back and raised his hands—

She hadn't felt any real interest in the gift, but his sharp glance at her hand drew her own gaze to what she held. It was a rainbow-filled sphere as transparent as crystal, as fragile as a bubble, and cool and smooth as a sphere of ice.

"And now," he cried, before she could react, "I bring you magic!"

The air exploded with colored lights, flashes of rainbow fire, and showers of sparks. Lord Lyon cried out involuntarily and threw up his arm to shield his eyes, dropping Ariella's hand.

She stepped away, clenched her fingers tightly on the magician's gift, and felt it shatter in her grasp.

A white-hot lance of fire pierced her from head to toe

until she thought she saw her own bones shining through the skin, and yet there was no pain—only the fire filling her, spreading through her veins, along her nerves, penetrating every part of her.

The weight of veil and golden band dropped from her head, and she stretched her chin upward—craned her neck up—

—and up, and up—

Her arms pulled in at her sides and grew shorter; her fingers stretched out longer and longer, fanning wide as they lengthened, skin weaving a web between them. The gown vanished, the undergown shredded, tore, became threads of gossamer flowing over her elongated fingers—

—became white feathers, clothing her powerful wings.

She was light! Lighter than a thistledown, light enough to—

:Fly, Wild Swan!: called a voice in her head. *:Fly! Fly for your freedom, fly and follow me!:*

Without thinking or wondering how, she launched herself into a sky still filled with showers of sparks and sheets of heatless flame. With powerful beats of her wings, she drove herself upwards, as beside her a swan as black as the deepest velvet matched her wingbeat for wingbeat. She was a swan, a huge swan whiter than snow, flying with strength she did not know she had.

In a moment, they were at the height of the towers. In two, they circled high above the castle roof. In three, they banked together off into the west. The figures of the wedding party below were as small as the painted people in an illumination, and one tiny scarlet-clad manikin gestured wildly and impotently in their direction.

But it was too late, for already they were beyond the reach of human or arrow. Perhaps, if someone had brought a goshawk out and set it after them, perhaps the powerful predatory bird would have caught one of them—but no one had, and in the fifth and sixth moments, they were gone, wings whistling in the chill air, speeding out of the sight of Lord Lyon and Lyon Castle forever.

The wild joy Ariella felt at that moment was only eclipsed by her incredulity as she tried to form her thoughts into words she hoped that her companion would hear.

:Merod?: she gasped, craning her head around on her long, graceful neck to look at him. He looked back at her, the mischief she remembered so well sparkling in his green eyes.

:I wondered how long it would take you to recognize me.: He chuckled.

:But—how? How did you know what happened? How did you find me? Why did you come for me?:

:Follow,: was all he said, and she did, flying until even her powerful wings tired, and he led her down to land on the chill waters of a remote wilderness lake.

He swam straight to the bank without stopping, and she followed in his wake. The moment their feet touched land, she felt a pang, a shiver ran through her, her vision blurred, and she found herself standing in shallow water, the remains of the samite undergown in rags about her.

The black-velvet-clad man lifted her by the waist and deposited her on the bank, wrapping his black cloak about her to shield her from the cold.

"You're—" she said, staring up into his green eyes, dumbfounded. "You're—not a riverhorse."

He chuckled. "Three gifts, my love. I was only mortal long enough to venture into that cold castle and pass your captor's tests. One wish to change, one wish to escape. Now I—we—are swan-folk, less Faerie than Kelpies, but not exactly children of Adam, either. We are swans upon the water and in the air, man and woman on the land, thanks to the Great One's gift."

"I thought you said you never had a reason to become a mortal—" was all she could say.

"I never had anyone I cared to share the other wishes

with, either—until now," was his reply, then he bent to kiss her mouth, and she melted into the kiss, and there was no reason to speak again for a very long time.

"Where are we going?" she asked when there was breath and reason to speak.

"Away," Merod replied and laughed. "Anywhere you like, beloved. We have all the world and the wings to take us there."

"Anywhere you like," she told him as he released her from his embrace to lead her into the water again. And as the cold water crept past her knees, she felt that shiver of power pass through her, and she was swimming at his side. *:Anywhere at all, so long as it is with you.:*

He arched up, wings flapping in triumph, as he trumpeted his pleasure. She echoed his triumph, and then they rose together into the air, wings beating together in time with their hearts, seeking the setting sun.

cool
food

MURDOCH BOOKS

Contents

Starters

Beetroot hummus

80 ml (⅓ cup) olive oil
1 onion, chopped
450 g tin baby beetroot, drained
220 g (1 cup) ready-made hummus
2 garlic cloves, crushed
1 tablespoon ground cumin
1–2 tablespoons lemon juice

Heat 1 tablespoon oil in a frying pan, add the onion and cook for 3 minutes, or until soft but not brown.

Place the onion, beetroot, hummus, garlic, cumin and lemon juice in a food processor and process the mixture until it is smooth.

Transfer to a serving bowl, season with salt and pepper to taste and drizzle with the remaining olive oil.

Makes 3 cups

Cheese and chilli shapes

155 g (1¼ cups) plain flour
pinch dry hot mustard
90 g butter, roughly chopped
60 g (½ cup) grated vintage Cheddar
   cheese
4 red chillies, seeded and sliced
1 egg yolk

Process the flour, mustard and butter until they resemble fine breadcrumbs. Add the cheese and chilli, then the egg yolk and 1 tablespoon water, and process until the mixture comes together. Gather into a ball, cover with plastic wrap and refrigerate for 30 minutes.

Preheat the oven to 190°C (375°F/ Gas 5). On a lightly floured surface, roll out the dough to a 5 mm thickness. Cut into 5 cm rounds.

Place on lightly greased baking trays and bake for 15–20 minutes, or until golden. Cool.

Makes 26

Tzatziki

2 Lebanese cucumbers
400 g Greek-style plain yoghurt
4 garlic cloves, crushed
3 tablespoons finely chopped mint,
  plus extra to garnish
1 tablespoon lemon juice

Cut the cucumbers in half lengthways, scoop out the seeds and discard. Leave the skin on and coarsely grate the cucumber into a small colander. Sprinkle with salt and leave over a large bowl for 15 minutes to drain off any bitter juices.

Meanwhile, place the yoghurt, crushed garlic, mint and lemon juice in a bowl, and stir until well combined.

Rinse the cucumber under cold water then, taking small handfuls, squeeze out any excess moisture. Combine the grated cucumber with the yoghurt mixture then season to taste with salt and freshly ground black pepper. Serve immediately or refrigerate until ready to serve, garnished with the extra mint.

Makes 2 cups

Note: Tzatziki is often served as a dip with flatbread or Turkish pide but is also suitable to serve as a sauce to accompany seafood and meat. Tzatziki will keep in an airtight container in the refrigerator for 2–3 days.

Tahini and chilli palmiers

135 g (½ cup) tahini
1 red chilli, seeded and finely
    chopped
½ teaspoon paprika
2 sheets ready-rolled puff pastry,
    thawed

Preheat the oven to 200°C (400°F/ Gas 6). Combine the tahini, chilli and paprika. Spread half the mixture over each sheet of pastry (to the edges).

Fold the pastry from opposite sides until the folds meet in the middle. Then fold one side over the other to resemble a closed book. Refrigerate for 5 minutes to firm.

Cut into 1.5 cm slices and place on baking trays lined with baking paper (leaving room for spreading).

Bake for 8 minutes, then turn over and bake for 2 minutes, or until golden brown.

Makes 36

Cheese fruit log

35 g (¼ cup) shelled pistachio nuts
250 g cream cheese, softened
50 g (¼ cup) finely chopped dried
  apricots
3 spring onions, finely chopped
45 g (¼ cup) sun-dried tomatoes,
  drained, finely chopped
10 g (⅓ cup) finely chopped flat-leaf
  parsley

Preheat the oven to 200°C (400°F/ Gas 6). Place the pistachio nuts on a lined baking tray and roast for 5 minutes, or until golden brown. Cool and finely chop.

Beat the cream cheese until smooth. Fold in the apricot, onion and sun-dried tomato, and pepper to taste.

Form the mixture into a 20 cm log. Roll the log in the combined pistachio nuts and parsley. Wrap in plastic wrap and refrigerate until firm.

Makes a 20 cm log

Dolmades

275 g vine leaves in brine
185 ml (¾ cup) olive oil
2 onions, finely chopped
·165 g (¾ cup) short-grain rice
6 spring onions, finely chopped
20 g (⅓ cup) chopped dill
1 tablespoon chopped mint
1 tablespoon lemon juice

lemon wedges

Rinse the vine leaves in cold water, soak in warm water for 1 hour and then drain.

Heat 125 ml (½ cup) of the oil in a large frying pan. Add the onion and cook over low heat for 5 minutes. Remove from the heat, cover and leave for 5 minutes. Add the rice, spring onion, herbs and lemon juice. Mix well and season.

Lay out a vine leaf, vein-side-up, on a plate. Place 3 teaspoons of filling onto the centre. Fold the sides over the mixture, then roll up towards the tip of the leaf. Repeat until you have made 42 dolmades.

Use five or six vine leaves to line the base of a large heavy-based pan. Pack the dolmades in the lined pan in two layers and drizzle with the remaining oil. Put a plate on top of the dolmades, to keep them in place, and cover with 375 ml (1½ cups) water. Bring to the boil, reduce the heat and simmer, covered, for 45 minutes. Remove the plate, lift out the dolmades with a slotted spoon. Serve either warm or cold with the lemon wedges.

Makes 42

Tapenade

400 g (2²/₃ cups) pitted Kalamata
olives
2 garlic cloves, crushed
2 anchovy fillets in oil, drained
2 tablespoons capers in brine, rinsed
and squeezed dry
2 teaspoons chopped fresh thyme
leaves
2 teaspoons Dijon mustard
1 tablespoon lemon juice
60 ml (¹/₄ cup) olive oil
1 tablespoon brandy, optional

Place the kalamata olives, crushed
garlic, anchovies, capers, chopped
thyme, Dijon mustard, lemon juice, oil
and brandy in a food processor and
process until smooth. Season to taste
with salt and freshly ground black
pepper. Spoon into a clean, warm jar,
cover with a layer of olive oil, seal and
refrigerate for up to 1 week. Serve on
bruschetta or with a meze plate.

Makes 1¹/₂ cups

Note: To make sure your storage jar
is very clean, preheat the oven to very
slow 120°C (250°F/Gas ¹/₂). Wash the
jar and lid thoroughly in hot soapy
water (or preferably in a dishwasher)
and rinse well with hot water. Put the
jar on a baking tray and place in the
oven for 20 minutes, or until fully dry
and you are ready to use it. Do not
dry the jar or lid with a tea towel.

Prawn san choy bau

1 kg raw medium prawns, peeled and
  deveined, or 500 g raw prawn meat
1 tablespoon oil
1 teaspoon sesame oil
2 spring onions, finely chopped
2 garlic cloves, crushed
1 cm x 2 cm piece fresh ginger,
  peeled and grated
120 g drained water chestnuts,
  chopped
1 tablespoon chopped red chilli
185 g (1 cup) cooked white rice
90 g (1 cup) bean sprouts, trimmed
25 g (½ cup) chopped coriander
  leaves
2 tablespoons soy sauce
2 tablespoons oyster sauce
2 tablespoons lime juice
60 ml (¼ cup) hoisin sauce

Wash the lettuce and separate the
leaves. Shake off any excess water
and drain on paper towels.

If the prawns are large, cut them into
smaller pieces. Heat a wok over high
heat, add the oils, swirl to coat, then
add the spring onion, crushed garlic
and ginger. Cook for 30 seconds then
add the prawn meat, water chestnuts
and chilli, season with salt and
cracked black pepper, and continue
stir-frying for 2 minutes. Add the
cooked rice, sprouts and coriander
and stir until combined.

Add the soy sauce, oyster sauce and
lime juice, then remove from the heat.
Transfer the mixture to a serving bowl.
Place the dry lettuce cups on a plate
and spoon the prawn mixture into
each one. Serve with hoisin sauce.

Serves 4–6

Potato, olive oil and garlic dip

460 g (2 cups) mashed potato
3 garlic cloves, crushed
185 ml (3/4 cup) olive oil
2 tablespoons white wine vinegar
5 tablespoons milk
30 g (1/2 cup) chopped fresh herbs

Combine the potato and garlic in a bowl. Using electric beaters, gradually beat in half the oil, then the vinegar, then the remaining oil.

Slowly beat in the milk. Add the herbs and season to taste with salt and freshly ground black pepper.

Makes 21/2 cups

Linseed crackers

125 g (1 cup) plain flour
½ teaspoon baking powder
½ teaspoon sugar
2 tablespoons linseeds
60 ml (¼ cup) milk
2 tablespoons olive oil

Preheat the oven to 200°C (400°F/ Gas 6). Process the flour, baking powder, sugar and ½ teaspoon salt. Add pepper to taste, and stir in the linseeds. Add the milk and oil and mix to form a wet crumbly mixture, adding extra milk if the mixture is too dry.

Turn the mixture out onto a flat, lightly floured surface and bring the mixture together into a ball.

Divide the mixture in half, place one half between two sheets of baking paper and roll out to a thickness of 2–3 mm. Prick liberally with a fork. Cut the dough into 12 irregular triangles and arrange in a single layer on a lightly greased baking tray. Repeat with the remaining dough.

Bake for 15–20 minutes, or until the bases are lightly golden. Turn over and bake for a further 4–5 minutes, or until the other side is also lightly golden. Transfer to a wire rack to cool completely.

Makes 24

Falafel

150 g (1 cup) dried split broad beans
    (see Note)
220 g (1 cup) dried chickpeas
1 onion, roughly chopped
6 garlic cloves, roughly chopped
2 teaspoons ground coriander
1 tablespoon ground cumin
15 g (½ cup) chopped flat-leaf parsley
¼ teaspoon chilli powder
½ teaspoon bicarbonate of soda
3 tablespoons chopped coriander
light oil, for deep-frying

Cover the broad beans with 750 ml (3 cups) water and leave to soak for 48 hours. (Drain the beans, rinse and cover with fresh water once or twice.) Place the chickpeas in a large bowl, cover with 750 ml (3 cups) water and soak for 12 hours.

Drain the beans and chickpeas and pat dry with paper towels. Process in a food processor with the onion and garlic until smooth.

Add the ground coriander, cumin, parsley, chilli powder, bicarbonate of soda and coriander. Season with salt and pepper, and mix until well combined. Transfer to a large bowl, knead and leave for 30 minutes.

Shape tablespoons of the mixture into balls, flatten slightly, place on a tray and leave for 20 minutes.

Fill a deep, heavy-based saucepan one-third full of oil and heat to 180°C (350°F), or until a cube of bread browns in 15 seconds. Cook the falafel in batches for 1–2 minutes, or until golden. Drain on paper towels. Serve with hummus, baba ghannouj and pitta bread.

Makes 30

Note: Split broad beans are available from specialist food stores.

Borek

400 g feta cheese
2 eggs, lightly beaten
25 g (¾ cup) chopped flat-leaf parsley
375 g filo pastry
80 ml (⅓ cup) olive oil

Preheat the oven to 180°C (350°F/ Gas 4). Lightly grease a baking tray. Crumble the feta into a large bowl using a fork or your fingers. Mix in the eggs and parsley and season with freshly ground black pepper.

Cover the filo pastry with a damp tea towel so it doesn't dry out. Remove one sheet at a time. Brushing each sheet lightly with olive oil, layer four sheets on top of one another. Cut the pastry into four 7 cm strips.

Place two rounded teaspoons of the feta mixture in one corner of each strip and fold diagonally, creating a triangle pillow. Place on the baking tray, seam-side-down, and brush with olive oil. Repeat with the remaining pastry and filling to make 24 parcels. Bake for 20 minutes, or until golden. Serve these as part of a meze plate.

Makes 24

Note: Fillings for borek are versatile and can be adapted to include your favourite cheeses such as haloumi, Gruyère, Cheddar or mozzarella.

Gravlax

1 teaspoon crushed black
  peppercorns
60 g (¼ cup) sugar
2 tablespoons coarse sea salt
2.5 kg salmon, filleted and boned
  but with the skin left on (ask your
  fishmonger to do this)
1 tablespoon vodka or brandy
4 tablespoons very finely chopped
  fresh dill

Mustard sauce
11/2 tablespoons cider vinegar
1 teaspoon caster sugar
125 ml (½ cup) olive oil
2 teaspoons chopped fresh dill
2 tablespoons Dijon mustard

Combine the peppercorns, sugar
and salt. Use tweezers to remove any
bones from the salmon. Pat dry with
paper towels and lay one fillet skin-
side-down in a tray. Sprinkle with half
the vodka, rub half the sugar mixture
into the flesh, then sprinkle with half
of the dill. Sprinkle the remaining
vodka over the second fillet and rub
the remaining sugar mixture into the
flesh. Lay it flesh-side-down on top
of the dill-coated salmon. Cover with
plastic wrap and place a heavy board
on top. Weigh the board downabnd
refrigerate for 24 hours, turning the
wrapped fillets over after 12 hours.

To make the mustard sauce, whisk
together the vinegar, sugar, oil, dill
and mustard, then cover until needed.

When the salmon is ready lift off
the top fillet and lay both fillets on
a board. Brush off the dill and any
seasoning mixture with a stiff pastry
brush. Sprinkle the fillets with the
remaining dill, pressing it onto the
salmon, then shake off any excess.
Serve the salmon whole, on the
serving board. Use a very sharp knife
with a flexible blade to thinly slice the
salmon on an angle towards the tail,
and serve with the mustard sauce
and dark rye bread.

Serves 20

Roast capsicum and eggplant spread

1 large (450 g) eggplant (aubergine),
  halved
2 teaspoons olive oil
1 red capsicum (pepper), halved
2 garlic cloves, crushed
15 g (¼ cup) chopped mint
3 teaspoons balsamic vinegar

Preheat the oven to 200°C (400°F/ Gas 6). Brush the cut side of the eggplant with some of the oil. Place cut-side-up on a baking tray. Brush the skin of the capsicum with the remaining oil and place skin-side-up on the baking tray next to the eggplant. Bake the eggplant and capsicum for about 30–35 minutes, or until the flesh is soft.

Place the capsicum in a plastic bag and leave to cool, then peel away the skin. Allow the eggplant to cool.

Scoop the flesh out of the eggplant and place in a food processor with the capsicum, garlic, mint and balsamic vinegar. Season to taste and process until smooth.

Makes 2 cups

Prawn pâté with garlic toasts

315 ml (1¼ cups) chicken stock
1 tablespoon gelatine
375 g cream cheese, at room
  temperature
800 g cooked prawns, peeled,
  deveined and roughly chopped
2 garlic cloves, crushed
2 tablespoons finely chopped chives
1 tablespoon chopped dill
30 g butter, melted
2 tablespoons olive oil
1 baguette, cut into 7 mm slices

Bring a shallow saucepan of water to the boil. Pour the stock into a heatproof bowl, then sprinkle the gelatine evenly over it; do not stir. Remove the saucepan from the heat and place the bowl of chicken stock in the pan. Stir the gelatine into the stock until it has dissolved; remove the bowl and cool for 30 minutes.

Place the gelatine liquid in a blender, add the cream cheese, half the prawn meat and half of the garlic and blend until smooth. Transfer to a bowl and leave for 20 minutes, or until thickened slightly.

Add the remaining prawn meat, chives and dill and season to taste. Pour into eight 125 ml (½ cup) ramekins. Cover with plastic wrap and refrigerate for 2 hours, or until set.

Preheat the oven to 180°C (350°F/ Gas 4). Combine the butter, oil and remaining garlic and lightly brush both sides of the bread slices with the mixture. Place apart on baking trays and bake for 10 minutes, or until golden and crisp. Leave to cool.

Unmould the pâté and serve with the garlic toasts.

Serves 8

Bruschetta

4 Roma (plum) tomatoes, chopped
80 ml (⅓ cup) olive oil
1 tablespoon balsamic vinegar
2 tablespoons chopped basil
8 slices day-old crusty Italian bread
1 garlic clove, peeled

chopped basil

Combine the tomatoes, olive oil, balsamic vinegar and chopped basil. Season well.

Toast the bread on one side. Rub the toasted side lightly with a peeled clove of garlic. Top with the tomato mixture and garnish with the extra chopped basil. Serve immediately.

Makes 8

Crunchy wedges

6 floury or all-purpose potatoes
1 tablespoon oil
25 g ($\frac{1}{4}$ cup) dry breadcrumbs
2 teaspoons chopped chives
1 teaspoon celery salt
$\frac{1}{4}$ teaspoon garlic powder
$\frac{1}{2}$ teaspoon chopped rosemary

Preheat the oven to 200°C (400°F/ Gas 6). Cut the potatoes into eight wedges each and toss in the oil.

Combine the breadcrumbs, chives, celery salt, garlic powder and rosemary in a bowl. Add the wedges and coat well. Place on greased baking trays and bake for 40 minutes, or until crisp and golden.

Makes 48

Chargrilled baby octopus

1 kg baby octopus
185 ml (¾ cup) red wine
2 tablespoons balsamic vinegar
2 tablespoons soy sauce
2 tablespoons hoisin sauce
1 garlic clove, crushed

Cut off the octopus heads, below the eyes, with a sharp knife. Discard the heads and guts. Push the beaks out with your index finger, remove and discard. Wash the octopus thoroughly under running water and drain on paper towels. If the octopus are very large, cut the tentacles into quarters.

Put the octopus in a large bowl. Stir together the wine, vinegar, soy sauce, hoisin sauce and garlic in a jug and pour over the octopus. Toss to coat, then cover and refrigerate for several hours, or overnight.

Heat a chargrill plate or barbecue hotplate until very hot and then lightly grease. Drain the octopus, reserving the marinade. Cook in batches for 3–5 minutes, or until the octopus flesh turns white. Brush the marinade over the octopus during cooking. Be careful not to overcook or the octopus will be tough. Serve warm or cold. Delicious with a green salad and lime wedges.

Serves 4

Chilled almond soup

1 loaf (200 g) day-old white Italian
bread, crust removed
155 g (1 cup) whole blanched
almonds
3–4 garlic cloves, chopped
125 ml (½ cup) extra virgin olive oil
80 ml (⅓ cup) sherry vinegar or white
wine vinegar
315–375 ml (1¼–1½ cups) vegetable
stock or water
2 tablespoons olive oil, extra
75 g day-old white Italian bread,
extra, crust removed and cut into
1 cm cubes
200 g small seedless green grapes

Soak the bread in cold water for
5 minutes, then squeeze to remove
any excess moisture. Place the
almonds and garlic in a food
processor and process until well
ground. Add the bread and process
to a smooth paste.

With the motor running, add the oil
in a slow steady stream until the
mixture is the consistency of thick
mayonnaise. Slowly add the sherry
vinegar and 315 ml (1¼ cups) of the
stock, or water, until the mixture has
reached the desired consistency.
Blend for 1 minute. Season with salt,
then refrigerate for at least 2 hours.
The soup thickens on refrigeration so
add more stock or water to reach the
desired consistency.

Heat the extra olive oil in a large frying
pan. Add the bread and toss over
medium heat for 2–3 minutes, or
until evenly golden brown. Drain on
crumpled paper towels. Serve the
soup very cold garnished with the
grapes and bread cubes.

Serves 4–6

Prawn, mango and macadamia salad

1 radicchio heart
25 g (½ cup) basil leaves, torn
30 g (1 cup) watercress sprigs
24 cooked king prawns, peeled
   and deveined with tails intact
3 tablespoons macadamia oil
3 tablespoons extra virgin olive oil
150 g (1 cup) macadamia nuts,
   coarsely chopped
2 garlic cloves, crushed
3 tablespoons lemon juice
1 ripe mango, cut into small dice

Remove the outer green leaves from the radicchio, leaving only the tender pink leaves. Tear any large leaves in half and arrange in a shallow serving bowl. Scatter with half of the basil leaves and the watercress, and toss lightly. Arrange the prawns over the salad leaves.

Heat the oils in a small, frying pan over medium heat. Add the nuts and cook for 5 minutes, or until golden. Add the garlic and cook for a further 30 seconds, then remove from the heat and add the lemon juice and mango. Season to taste, pour over the salad and scatter with the remaining basil leaves.

Serves 4–6

Pear and walnut salad with lime vinaigrette

1 small baguette, cut into 16 thin
  slices
oil, for brushing
1 garlic clove, cut in half
100 g (1 cup) walnuts
200 g ricotta cheese
400 g mixed salad leaves
2 pears, cut into 2 cm cubes, mixed
  with 2 tablespoons lime juice

Lime vinaigrette
60 ml (¼ cup) lime juice
3 tablespoons oil
2 tablespoons raspberry vinegar

Preheat the oven to 180°C (350°F/
Gas 4). Brush the baguette slices with
a little oil, rub with the cut side of the
garlic, then place on a baking tray.
Bake for 10 minutes, or until crisp
and golden. Place the walnuts on a
baking tray and roast for 5–8 minutes,
or until slightly browned — shake the
tray to ensure even colouring. Allow
to cool for 5 minutes.

To make the lime vinaigrette, whisk
together the lime juice, oil, vinegar,
1 teaspoon salt and ½ teaspoon
freshly ground black pepper in a small
bowl. Set aside until ready to use.

Spread some of the ricotta cheese on
each crouton, then cook under a hot
grill for 2–3 minutes, or until hot.

Place the mixed salad, pears and
walnuts in a bowl, add the vinaigrette
and toss through. Divide the salad
among four serving bowls and serve
with the ricotta cheese croutons.

Serves 4

Prawns with saffron potatoes

16 raw medium prawns
80 ml (⅓ cup) olive oil
450 g new potatoes, cut in half
¼ teaspoon saffron threads, crushed
1 garlic clove, crushed
1 bird's eye chilli, seeded and finely
  chopped
1 teaspoon grated lime zest
60 ml (¼ cup) lime juice
200 g baby rocket

Preheat the oven to 180°C (350°F/ Gas 4). Peel and devein the prawns, leaving the tails intact.

Heat 2 tablespoons of the oil in a frying pan and brown the potatoes. Transfer to a roasting tin and toss gently with the saffron and some salt and black pepper. Bake for 25 minutes, or until tender.

Heat a chargrill pan over medium heat. Toss the prawns with the garlic, chilli, lime zest and 1 tablespoon of the oil in a small bowl. Grill the prawns for 2 minutes each side, or until pink and cooked.

In a small jar, shake the lime juice and the remaining oil. Season with salt and pepper. Place the potatoes on a plate, top with the rocket and prawns and drizzle with dressing.

Serves 4

Salmon carpaccio

3 vine-ripened tomatoes
1 tablespoon baby capers, rinsed
   and drained
1 tablespoon chopped dill
500 g sashimi salmon
1 tablespoon extra virgin olive oil
1 tablespoon lime juice

ciabatta bread

Cut a cross in the base of the tomatoes. Place in a bowl and cover with boiling water. Leave to stand for 2–3 minutes, or until the skin blisters. Drain, plunge into cold water, then drain and peel. Cut the tomatoes in half, scoop out the seeds with a teaspoon and dice the flesh. Place in a bowl and stir in the capers and dill.

Using a very sharp knife, carefully slice the salmon into paper-thin slices, cutting across the grain. Divide the salmon equally among four plates, arranging in a single layer.

Place a mound of the tomato mixture in the centre of each plate. Whisk together the olive oil and lime juice, and season with salt. Drizzle over the tomato and salmon, and season with black pepper. Serve immediately with ciabatta bread.

Serves 4

Artichoke, prosciutto and rocket salad

4 artichokes
2 eggs, lightly beaten
20 g (¼ cup) fresh breadcrumbs
25 g (¼ cup) grated Parmesan
  cheese
olive oil for frying, plus 1 tablespoon
  extra
8 slices prosciutto
3 teaspoons white wine vinegar
1 garlic clove, crushed
150 g rocket, long stalks trimmed

shaved Parmesan cheese (optional)
sea salt

Bring a large saucepan of water to the boil. Remove the hard, outer leaves of each artichoke, trim the stem and cut 2–3 cm off the top. Cut into quarters and remove the furry 'choke'. Boil the pieces for 2 minutes, then drain.

Whisk the eggs in a bowl and combine the seasoned breadcrumbs and grated Parmesan in another bowl. Dip each artichoke quarter into the egg, then roll in the crumb mixture to coat. Fill a frying pan with olive oil to a depth of 2 cm and heat over medium–high heat. Add the artichokes in batches and fry for 2–3 minutes, or until golden. Remove from the pan and drain on paper towels.

Heat 1 tablespoon of olive oil in a non-stick frying pan over medium–high heat. Cook the prosciutto in two batches for 2 minutes, or until crisp and golden. Remove from the pan, reserving the oil.

Combine the reserved oil, vinegar and garlic with a little salt and pepper. Place the rocket in a bowl, add half of the salad dressing and toss well. Divide the rocket, artichokes and prosciutto among four plates, and drizzle with the remaining dressing. Garnish with shaved Parmesan, if desired, and sprinkle with sea salt.

Serves 4

Prawn millefeuille

Lemon mayonnaise
1 egg yolk
½ teaspoon Dijon mustard
pinch of sugar
1 teaspoon cider vinegar
1 teaspoon finely grated lemon zest
1 tablespoon lemon juice
185 ml (¾ cup) oil

2 sheets ready-rolled frozen puff
   pastry, thawed
750 g cooked medium prawns
75 g rocket, torn
½ small red onion, thinly sliced into
   rings
2 tablespoons capers, rinsed
   and drained
1 tablespoon chopped flat-leaf
   parsley

Preheat the oven to 200°C (400°F/ Gas 6) and line two baking trays with baking paper. To make the lemon mayonnaise, combine the egg yolk, mustard, sugar, vinegar, lemon zest and juice in a bowl. Gradually add the oil, at first drop by drop, then in a thin steady stream, beating continuously with a whisk or wooden spoon until it thickens. Season.

Cut the pastry sheets into quarters, then place well apart on the baking trays. Bake for about 15 minutes, or until golden and puffed. Cool for 2 minutes before lifting with a spatula onto a wire rack to cool.

Peel and devein the prawns, then cut them in half lengthways. Using half the rocket, prawns, onion rings and capers, make a neat pile on four serving plates and drizzle with some of the mayonnaise. Place a piece of pastry over the salad, then add the remaining ingredients, including some mayonnaise, on top of the pastry square. Finish with another piece of pastry, sprinkle with parsley and serve.

Serves 4

Haloumi with salad and garlic bread

4 firm, ripe tomatoes
1 Lebanese cucumber
140 g rocket
80 g (½ cup) Kalamata olives
1 loaf crusty unsliced white bread
5 tablespoons olive oil
1 large garlic clove, cut in half
400 g haloumi cheese
1 tablespoon lemon juice
1 tablespoon chopped oregano

Preheat the oven to 180°C (350°F/ Gas 4). Heat the grill to high.

Cut the tomatoes and cucumber into bite-sized chunks and place in a serving dish with the rocket and olives. Mix well.

Slice the bread into eight 1.5 cm slices, drizzle 1½ tablespoons of the olive oil over the bread and season with salt and pepper. Grill until lightly golden, then rub each slice thoroughly with a cut side of the garlic. Wrap the bread loosely in foil and keep warm in the oven.

Cut the haloumi into eight slices. Heat ½ tablespoon of the oil in a shallow frying pan and fry the haloumi slices for 1–2 minutes on each side, until crisp and golden brown.

Whisk together the lemon juice, oregano and remaining olive oil to use as a dressing. Season, to taste. Pour half the dressing over the salad and toss well. Arrange the haloumi on top and drizzle with dressing. Serve immediately with the warm garlic bread.

Serves 4

Baked ricotta and red capsicum with pesto

1 large red capsicum (pepper), cut
  into quarters and seeded
750 g low-fat ricotta cheese
1 egg
6 slices wholegrain bread

Pesto
2 tablespoons pine nuts
100 g (2 cups) basil
2 garlic cloves
2 tablespoons good-quality olive oil
2 tablespoons finely grated Parmesan
  cheese

Grill the capsicum, skin-side-up, under a hot grill for 5–6 minutes, or until the skin blackens and blisters. Place in a bowl and cover with plastic wrap until cool. Peel off the skin and slice the flesh into 2 cm wide strips.

To make the pesto, place the pine nuts, basil and garlic in a food processor and process for 15 seconds, or until finely chopped. While the processor is running, add the oil in a continuous thin stream, then season with salt and pepper. Stir in the Parmesan.

Preheat the oven to 180°C (350°F/ Gas 4). Grease six large muffin holes.

Mix the ricotta and egg until well combined. Season with salt and freshly ground black pepper. Divide the capsicum strips among the muffin holes, top with 2 teaspoons pesto and spoon in the ricotta mixture.

Bake for 35–40 minutes, or until the ricotta is firm and golden. Cool, then unmould. Toast the bread slices and cut them into fingers. Serve with the baked ricotta and the remaining pesto on the side.

Serves 6

Scallop salad with saffron dressing

pinch saffron threads
60 g (¼ cup) mayonnaise
1½ tablespoons cream
1 teaspoon lemon juice
20 scallops (500 g) with roe
  attached
25 g butter
1 tablespoon olive oil
100 g mixed salad leaves
4 g (⅓ cup) chervil leaves

To make the dressing, place the saffron threads in a bowl and soak in 2 teaspoons of hot water for 10 minutes. Add the mayonnaise, mixing well, until it is a rich yellow in colour. Stir in the cream, then the lemon juice. Refrigerate until needed.

Make sure the scallops are clean of digestive tract before cooking. Heat the butter and olive oil in a large frying pan over high heat and sear the scallops in small batches for 1 minute on each side.

Divide the mixed salad leaves and chervil among four serving plates, then top each with five scallops. Drizzle the dressing over the scallops and the salad leaves before serving.

Serves 4

Orange, goat's cheese and hazelnut salad

20 g hazelnuts
1 tablespoon orange juice
1 tablespoon lemon juice
125 ml (½ cup) olive oil
250 g watercress, well rinsed and dried
50 g baby English spinach leaves, well rinsed and dried
24 orange segments
300 g firm goat's cheese, sliced into 4 equal portions

Preheat the oven to 180°C (350°F/ Gas 4). Put the hazelnuts on a tray and roast for 5–6 minutes, or until the skin turns dark brown. Wrap the hazelnuts in a clean tea towel and rub them together to remove the skins.

Combine the nuts, orange juice, lemon juice and a pinch of salt in a food processor. With the motor running, gradually add the oil a few drops at a time. When about half the oil has been added, pour in the remainder in a steady stream.

Remove the stems from the watercress and place the leaves in a bowl with the spinach, orange segments and 2 tablespoons of the dressing. Toss to combine and season to taste with pepper. Arrange the salad on four plates.

Heat a small, non-stick frying pan over medium–high heat and brush lightly with olive oil. When hot, carefully press each slice of goat's cheese firmly into the pan and cook for 1–2 minutes, or until a crust has formed on the cheese. Carefully remove the cheese from the pan and arrange over the salads, crust-side-up. Drizzle the remaining dressing over the salads.

Serves 4

Prawn cocktails

Cocktail sauce
250 g (1 cup) whole-egg mayonnaise
60 ml (¼ cup) tomato sauce
2 teaspoons Worcestershire sauce
½ teaspoon lemon juice
1 drop Tabasco sauce

1 kg cooked medium prawns

lettuce leaves
lemon wedges
sliced bread

For the cocktail sauce, mix all the ingredients together in a bowl and season with salt and pepper.

Peel the prawns, leaving some with their tails intact to use as a garnish. Remove the tails from the rest. Gently pull out the dark vein from each prawn back, starting at the head end. Add the prawns without tails to the sauce and mix to coat.

Arrange lettuce in serving dishes or bowls. Spoon some prawns into each dish. Garnish with the reserved prawns, drizzling with some dressing. Serve with lemon wedges and bread.

Serves 6

Note: If you wish, you can make the cocktail sauce several hours ahead and store it in the refrigerator. Stir in 2 tablespoons of thick (double) cream for a creamier sauce.

Red gazpacho

1 kg vine-ripened tomatoes
2 slices day-old white Italian bread,
    crust removed, broken into pieces
1 red capsicum (pepper), seeded and
    roughly chopped
2 garlic cloves, chopped
1 small green chilli, chopped, optional
1 teaspoon sugar
2 tablespoons red wine vinegar
2 tablespoons extra virgin olive oil
8 ice cubes

Garnish
1/2 Lebanese cucumber, seeded and
    finely diced
1/2 red capsicum (pepper), seeded
    and finely diced
1/2 green capsicum (pepper), seeded
    and finely diced
1/2 red onion, finely diced
1/2 tomato, diced

Score a cross in the base of each tomato. Place in a bowl of boiling water for 1 minute, then plunge into cold water and peel away from the cross. Cut the tomatoes in half, scoop out the seeds and chop the flesh.

Soak the bread in cold water for 5 minutes, then squeeze out any excess liquid. Place the bread in a food processor with the tomato, capsicum, garlic, chilli, sugar and vinegar, and process until smooth.

With the motor running, add the oil to make a smooth mixture. Season with salt and ground black pepper. Refrigerate for at least 2 hours. Add a little extra vinegar, if desired.

To make the garnish, place all the ingredients in a bowl and mix well. Serve the soup in bowls with two ice cubes in each bowl. Spoon the garnish into separate bowls.

Serves 4

Scallops, ginger and spinach salad

300 g scallops, without roe
100 g (2 cups) baby English spinach
  leaves
1 small red capsicum (pepper), cut
  into very fine strips
50 g bean sprouts
25 ml sake
1 tablespoon lime juice
2 teaspoons shaved palm sugar
  or soft brown sugar
1 teaspoon fish sauce

Remove any membrane or hard white muscle from the scallops. Lightly brush a chargrill plate with oil. Cook the scallops in batches on the chargrill plate for 1 minute each side, or until cooked.

Divide the spinach, capsicum and bean sprouts among four plates. Arrange the scallops over the top.

To make the dressing, place the sake, lime juice, palm sugar and fish sauce in a small bowl, and mix together well. Pour over the salad and serve immediately.

Serves 4

Asparagus with smoked salmon and hollandaise

175 g butter
4 egg yolks
1 tablespoon lime juice
4 eggs, at room temperature
310 g asparagus spears
200 g smoked salmon
shaved Parmesan cheese

Melt the butter in a small saucepan and skim any froth from the surface. Remove from the heat. In a separate saucepan, mix the egg yolks with 2 tablespoons water. Place over very low heat and whisk for 30 seconds, or until pale and foamy, then continue whisking for 2–3 minutes, or until the whisk leaves a trail — do not overheat the eggs will scramble. Remove from the heat. Add the cooled butter a little at a time, whisking well between each addition. Avoid using the milky whey at the bottom of the pan. Stir in the lime juice and season. If the sauce is still runny, return to the heat and whisk vigorously until thick, taking care not to scramble.

Half fill a saucepan with water and add the eggs. Bring to the boil and cook for 6–7 minutes, stirring occasionally to centre the yolks. Drain and cool, then peel and quarter.

Bring a large saucepan of lightly salted water to the boil. Add the asparagus and cook for 3 minutes, or until just tender. Drain and pat dry. Divide the asparagus and smoked salmon among four serving plates. Arrange the eggs over the top. Spoon on the hollandaise and top with the Parmesan. Season and serve.

Serves 4

Haloumi and asparagus salad with salsa verde

250 g haloumi cheese
380 g small, thin asparagus spears
2 tablespoons garlic oil
7 g (1/4 cup) basil leaves
10 g (1/2 cup) mint leaves
20 g (1 cup) parsley leaves
2 tablespoons baby capers rinsed
  and drained
1 garlic clove
2 tablespoons olive oil
1 tablespoon lemon juice
1 tablespoon lime juice
2 handfuls mixed salad leaves

Heat a chargrill pan over medium heat. Cut the haloumi into 1 cm slices and cut each slice in half diagonally to make two small triangles. Brush the haloumi and asparagus with the garlic oil. Chargrill the asparagus for 1 minute or until just tender, and the haloumi until grill marks appear and it is warmed through. Keep warm.

To make the salsa verde, place the herbs, capers, garlic and oil in a food processor and blend until smooth. Add the juices, and pulse briefly.

Divide the salad leaves among four serving plates. Top with the haloumi and asparagus, and drizzle with a little salsa verde.

Serves 4

Sweet citrus scallop salad

Lemon and herb dressing
½ preserved lemon
60 ml (¼ cup) olive oil
2 tablespoons lemon juice
1 tablespoon sweet chilli sauce
2 tablespoons white wine vinegar
2 tablespoons chopped coriander

500 g potatoes
oil, for shallow-frying
750 g scallops, without roe
2 tablespoons olive oil, extra
75 g baby English spinach leaves

For the dressing, scoop out and discard the pulp from the preserved lemon, wash the skin and cut into thin slices. Put in a bowl and whisk with the olive oil, lemon juice, sweet chilli sauce, wine vinegar and coriander.

Cut the potatoes into paper-thin slices. Heat 2 cm oil in a deep heavy-based frying pan and cook batches of the potato for 1–2 minutes, or until crisp and golden. Drain on crumpled paper towels.

Slice or pull off any membrane, vein or hard white muscle from the scallops. Heat the extra oil in a frying pan over high heat and cook the scallops in batches for 1–2 minutes, or until they are golden brown on both sides.

Divide half the spinach among four plates. Top with potato, then half the scallops and more spinach. Finish with more scallops. Drizzle with the dressing just before serving.

Serves 4

Smoked salmon and rocket salad

Dressing
1 tablespoon extra virgin olive oil
2 tablespoons balsamic vinegar

150 g rocket
1 avocado
250 g smoked salmon
325 g jar marinated goat's cheese,
    drained and crumbled
2 tablespoons roasted hazelnuts,
    coarsely chopped

For the dressing, thoroughly whisk together the oil and vinegar in a bowl. Season, to taste.

Trim any long stems from the rocket, rinse, pat dry and gently toss in a bowl with the dressing.

Cut the avocado in half lengthways, then cut each half lengthways into six wedges. Discard the skin and place three wedges on each serving plate and arrange a pile of rocket over the top.

Drape pieces of salmon over the rocket. Scatter the cheese and nuts over the top and season with ground black pepper. Serve immediately.

Serves 4

Note: A whole smoked trout can be used instead of the salmon. Peel, remove the bones, then break the flesh into bite-sized pieces.

Vietnamese prawn salad

1 small Chinese cabbage, finely
  shredded
60 g (¼ cup) sugar
60 ml (¼ cup) fish sauce
80 ml (⅓ cup) lime juice
1 tablespoon white vinegar
1 small red onion, finely sliced
750 g fresh cooked tiger prawns,
  peeled and deveined, tails intact
30 g (⅔ cup) chopped coriander
  leaves
30 g (⅔ cup) chopped Vietnamese
  mint leaves

Vietnamese mint leaves

Place the Chinese cabbage in a large
bowl, cover with plastic wrap and chill
for 30 minutes.

Put the sugar, fish sauce, lime juice,
vinegar and ½ teaspoon salt in a
small jug and mix well.

Toss together the shredded cabbage,
onion, prawns, coriander, mint and
dressing, and garnish with the extra
mint leaves.

Serves 6

Note: Vietnamese mint is available
from Asian grocery stores.

Mains

Lamb with roasted tomatoes

1 tablespoon red wine vinegar
½ Lebanese cucumber, finely diced
100 g Greek-style yoghurt
2 teaspoons chopped mint
½ teaspoon ground cumin
80 ml (⅓ cup) olive oil
6 vine-ripened tomatoes
4 garlic cloves, finely chopped
1 tablespoon chopped oregano
1 tablespoon chopped parsley
600 g asparagus spears, trimmed
2 lamb backstraps or fillets (500 g)

Combine the vinegar, cucumber, yoghurt, chopped mint, cumin and 1 tablespoon of olive oil in a small jug.

Preheat the oven to 180°C (350°F/ Gas 4). Cut the tomatoes in half and scoop out the seeds. Combine the garlic, oregano and parsley, and sprinkle into the tomato shells.

Place the tomatoes on a rack in a baking tin. Drizzle them with 1 tablespoon of the olive oil and roast for 1 hour. Remove from the oven, cut each piece in half again and keep warm. Place the asparagus in the roasting tin, drizzle with another tablespoon of olive oil, season and roast for 10 minutes.

Meanwhile, heat the remaining oil in a frying pan. Season the lamb well and cook over medium–high heat for 5 minutes on each side, then set aside to rest.

Remove the asparagus from the oven and arrange on a serving plate. Top with the tomato. Slice the lamb on the diagonal and arrange on top of the tomato. Drizzle with the dressing and serve immediately.

Serves 4

Indian marinated chicken salad

60 ml (¼ cup) lemon juice
1½ teaspoons garam masala
1 teaspoon ground turmeric
1 tablespoon finely grated fresh
  ginger
2 garlic cloves, finely chopped
3½ tablespoons vegetable oil
3 chicken breast fillets (650 g)
1 onion, thinly sliced
2 zucchini (courgettes), thinly sliced
  on the diagonal
100 g watercress leaves
150 g freshly shelled peas
2 ripe tomatoes, finely chopped
30 g (1 cup) coriander leaves

Dressing
1 teaspoon cumin seeds
½ teaspoon coriander seeds
90 g (⅓ cup) natural yoghurt
2 tablespoons chopped mint
2 tablespoons lemon juice

Combine the lemon juice, garam masala, turmeric, ginger, garlic and 2 teaspoons oil in a large bowl. Add the chicken fillets and onion, toss to coat in the marinade, cover, and refrigerate for 1 hour.

Remove and discard the onion then heat 2 tablespoons of oil in a large, frying pan. Cook the chicken for about 4–5 minutes on each side or until it is cooked through. Remove the chicken from the pan and leave for 5 minutes. Cut each breast across the grain into 1 cm slices.

Heat the remaining oil in the pan and cook the zucchini for 2 minutes, or until lightly golden and tender. Toss with the watercress in a large bowl. Cook the peas in boiling water for 5 minutes, or until tender, then drain. Rinse under cold water to cool. Add to the salad with the tomato, chicken and coriander.

For the dressing, gently roast the cumin and coriander seeds in a dry frying pan for 1–2 minutes, or until fragrant. Remove, then pound the seeds to a powder. Mix with the yoghurt, mint and lemon juice, then gently fold through the salad.

Serves 4

White bean salad with tuna

200 g (1 cup) dried cannellini beans
  (see Note)
2 fresh bay leaves
1 large garlic clove, smashed
350 g green beans, trimmed
2 baby fennel bulbs, thinly sliced
½ small red onion, very thinly sliced
30 g (1 cup) parsley leaves, roughly
  chopped
1 tablespoon olive oil
2 fresh tuna fillets (400 g)
80 ml (⅓ cup) lemon juice
1 garlic clove, extra, finely chopped
1 red chilli, seeds removed, finely
  chopped
1 teaspoon sugar
1 tablespoon lemon zest
125 ml (½ cup) extra virgin olive oil

Put the beans in a bowl, cover with cold water, allowing room for the beans to expand, and leave for at least 8 hours.

Rinse the beans well and transfer them to a saucepan. Cover with cold water, add the torn bay leaves and smashed garlic, and simmer for 20–25 minutes, or until tender. Drain.

Cook the green beans in boiling water for 1–2 minutes, or until tender, and refresh under cold water. Mix with the fennel, onion and parsley.

Heat the oil in a large, heavy-based frying pan and cook the tuna fillets over high heat for 2 minutes on each side or until still pink in the centre. Remove, rest for 2–3 minutes, then cut into 3 cm chunks. Add to the green bean mixture with the cannellini beans and toss to combine.

Combine the lemon juice, garlic, chilli, sugar and lemon zest. Whisk in the olive oil and season with salt and pepper. Toss gently through the salad.

Serves 4–6

Note: You may substitute a 425 g tin of cooked cannellini beans for the dried beans. Rinse and drain well before using — they will not require any further preparation.

Minced pork and noodle salad

1 tablespoon peanut oil
500 g minced pork
2 garlic cloves, finely chopped
1 stalk lemon grass, finely chopped
2–3 red Asian shallots, thinly sliced
3 teaspoons finely grated fresh ginger
1 small red chilli, finely chopped
5 fresh kaffir lime leaves, very finely
  shredded
170 g glass (mung bean) noodles
60 g baby English spinach leaves
50 g (1 cup) roughly chopped
  coriander
170 g peeled, finely chopped fresh
  pineapple
10 g (½ cup) mint leaves
1½ tablespoons shaved palm sugar
  or soft brown sugar
2 tablespoons fish sauce
80 ml (⅓ cup) lime juice
2 teaspoons sesame oil
2 teaspoons peanut oil, extra

Heat a wok until very hot, add the peanut oil and swirl to coat the wok. Add the pork and stir-fry in batches over high heat for 5 minutes, or until lightly golden. Add the garlic, lemon grass, shallots, grated ginger, chilli and lime leaves, and stir-fry for a further 1–2 minutes, or until fragrant.

Place the noodles in a large bowl and cover with boiling water for 30 seconds, or until softened. Rinse under cold water and drain well. Toss in a bowl with the spinach, coriander, pineapple, mint and pork mixture.

To make the dressing, mix together the palm sugar, fish sauce and lime juice. Add the sesame oil and extra peanut oil, and whisk to combine. Toss through the salad and season with freshly ground black pepper.

Serves 4

Warm chicken and pasta salad

375 g penne
100 ml olive oil
4 long, thin eggplants (aubergines),
   thinly sliced on the diagonal
2 chicken breast fillets
2 teaspoons lemon juice
15 g (1/2 cup) chopped flat-leaf parsley
270 g chargrilled red capsicum
   (pepper), drained and sliced
   (see Note)
155 g fresh asparagus spears,
   trimmed, blanched and cut into
   5 cm lengths
85 g semi-dried (sun-blushed)
   tomatoes, finely sliced

grated Parmesan cheese (optional)

Cook the pasta in a large saucepan of boiling water until *al dente*. Drain, return to the pan and keep warm. Heat 2 tablespoons of the oil in a large frying pan over high heat and cook the eggplant for 4–5 minutes, or until golden and cooked through.

Heat a lightly oiled chargrill pan over high heat and cook the chicken for 5 minutes each side, or until browned and cooked through. Cut into thick slices. Combine the lemon juice, parsley and the remaining oil in a small jar and shake well. Return the pasta to the heat, toss through the dressing, chicken, eggplant, capsicum, asparagus and tomato until well mixed and warmed through. Season with black pepper. Serve warm with a scattering of grated Parmesan, if desired.

Serves 4

Note: Jars of chargrilled capsicum can be bought at the supermarket; otherwise, visit your local deli.

Greek peppered lamb salad

300 g lamb backstraps or fillets
1½ tablespoons black pepper
3 vine-ripened tomatoes, cut into
    8 wedges
2 Lebanese cucumbers, sliced
150 g lemon and garlic marinated
    Kalamata olives, drained (reserving
    1½ tablespoons oil)
100 g Greek feta cheese, cubed
¾ teaspoon dried oregano
1 tablespoon lemon juice
1 tablespoon extra virgin olive oil

Roll the backstraps in the pepper, pressing the pepper on with your fingers. Cover and refrigerate for 15 minutes.

Place the tomato, cucumber, olives, feta and ½ teaspoon of the dried oregano in a bowl.

Heat a chargrill pan or barbecue plate, brush with oil and when very hot, cook the lamb for 2–3 minutes on each side, or until cooked to your liking. Keep warm.

Whisk the lemon juice, extra virgin olive oil, reserved Kalamata oil and the remaining dried oregano together well. Season. Pour half the dressing over the salad, toss together and arrange on a serving platter.

Cut the lamb on the diagonal into 1 cm thick slices and arrange on top of the salad. Pour the remaining dressing on top and serve.

Serves 4

Chargrilled chicken with spinach and raspberries

60 ml (¼ cup) raspberry vinegar
2 tablespoons lime juice
2 garlic cloves, crushed
2 tablespoons chopped oregano
1 teaspoon soft brown sugar
2 small red chillies, finely chopped
125 ml (½ cup) virgin olive oil
4 chicken breast fillets
1 teaspoon Dijon mustard
200 g baby English spinach leaves
250 g fresh raspberries

Mix 2 tablespoons of the raspberry vinegar, the lime juice, crushed garlic, 1 tablespoon of the oregano, the sugar, chilli and 60 ml (¼ cup) of the oil in a large bowl. Immerse the chicken in the marinade, cover and refrigerate for 2 hours.

Preheat the oven to 180°C (350°F/ Gas 4). Heat a chargrill pan and cook the chicken for 3 minutes on each side, then place on a baking tray and bake for a further 5 minutes, or until cooked through. Allow the chicken to rest for 5 minutes, then cut each breast into five strips on the diagonal.

To make the dressing, combine the remaining oil, vinegar and oregano with the mustard, ¼ teaspoon salt and freshly ground black pepper and mix well. Toss the spinach and raspberries with half of the dressing. Top with the chicken and drizzle with the remaining dressing.

Serves 4

Fusilli salad with sherry vinaigrette

300 g fusilli
250 g (2 cups) cauliflower florets
125 ml (½ cup) olive oil
16 slices pancetta
10 g (½ cup) small sage leaves
100 g (⅔ cup) pine nuts, toasted
2 tablespoons finely chopped Asian
  shallots
1½ tablespoons sherry vinegar
1 small red chilli, finely chopped
2 garlic cloves, crushed
1 teaspoon soft brown sugar
2 tablespoons orange juice
15 g (¼ cup) parsley, finely chopped
35 g (⅓ cup) shaved Parmesan
  cheese

Cook the fusilli in a large saucepan of rapidly boiling, salted water for 12 minutes, or until *al dente*. Drain and refresh under cold water until it is cool. Drain well. Blanch the cauliflower florets in boiling water for 3 minutes, then drain and cool.

Heat 1 tablespoon of olive oil in a non-stick frying pan and cook the pancetta for 2 minutes or until crisp. Drain on crumpled paper towels. Add 1 more tablespoon of oil and cook the sage leaves for 1 minute or until crisp. Drain on crumpled paper towels. In a large serving bowl, combine the pasta, pine nuts and cauliflower.

Heat the remaining olive oil, add the shallots and cook gently for 2 minutes, or until soft. Remove from the heat then add the vinegar, chilli, garlic, brown sugar, orange juice and chopped parsley. Pour the warm dressing over the pasta and toss gently to combine.

Place the salad in a serving bowl. Crumble the pancetta over the top and scatter with sage leaves and shaved Parmesan. Serve warm.

Serves 6

Prawn tacos

2 firm ripe tomatoes, seeded and
  diced
2 tablespoons lime juice
½ teaspoon chilli powder
½ teaspoon ground cumin
2 tablespoons oil
1 red onion, diced
4 garlic cloves, crushed
18 raw medium prawns, peeled,
  deveined and roughly chopped
3 tablespoons chopped flat-leaf
  parsley
8 corn taco shells
150 g shredded iceberg lettuce
1 avocado, diced
125 g (½ cup) sour cream

Preheat the oven to 180°C (350°F/
Gas 4). Combine the tomato, lime
juice, chilli powder and cumin.

Heat the oil in a frying pan, add the
onion and garlic and cook gently for
3–5 minutes, or until soft. Add the
prawns and toss briefly, then stir
in the tomato mixture and cook
for another 3–5 minutes, or until
the prawns are pink and cooked. Stir
in the parsley. Meanwhile, heat the
taco shells on a baking tray in the
oven for 5 minutes.

Place some lettuce in the bottom
of each taco shell, then fill with
the prawn mixture. Top with some
avocado and a dollop of sour cream.

Serves 4

Warm pork salad with blue cheese croutons

125 ml (½ cup) olive oil
1 large garlic clove, crushed
400 g pork fillet, cut into 5 mm slices
1 small or ½ a large baguette, cut
  into 20 x 5 mm slices
100 g blue cheese, crumbled
2 tablespoons sherry vinegar
½ teaspoon soft brown sugar
150 g mixed salad leaves

Place the olive oil and garlic in a jar and shake well. Heat 2 teaspoons of the garlic oil in a frying pan, add half the pork and cook for 1 minute on each side. Remove and keep warm. Add another 2 teaspoons garlic oil and cook the remaining pork. Remove. Season the pork with salt and black pepper to taste.

Lay the bread slices on a baking tray and brush with a little garlic oil on one side. Cook the bread under a hot grill until golden. Turn the bread over, sprinkle with the crumbled blue cheese, then return to the grill and cook until the cheese has melted (this will happen very quickly).

Add the sherry vinegar and sugar to the remaining garlic oil and shake well. Place the salad leaves in a large bowl, add the pork and pour on the salad dressing. Toss well. Place a mound of salad in the middle of four serving plates and arrange five croutons around the edge of each salad. Serve the salad immediately.

Serves 4

Thai beef salad

600 g beef fillet, trimmed
125 ml (½ cup) fish sauce
1 tablespoon peanut oil
1 small dried red chilli, roughly
  chopped
4 Asian shallots, finely sliced
2 spring onions, thinly sliced on an
  angle
4 tablespoons mint leaves
4 tablespoons coriander leaves
1 garlic clove, crushed
100 ml lime juice
2 teaspoons grated palm sugar or
  soft brown sugar
2 vine-ripened tomatoes, each cut
  into 8 wedges
100 g butter lettuce, washed and
  trimmed

Place the beef fillet in a bowl with
2 tablespoons of fish sauce. Cover
and chill for 3 hours, turning the
meat several times.

Place a baking tray in the oven and
preheat to 220°C (425°F/ Gas 7).
Heat the oil in a frying pan over
high heat and cook the beef fillet
for 1 minute on each side, or until
browned, then roast for 15 minutes,
or until medium–rare. Remove from
the oven and rest for 10 minutes.

Meanwhile, place the chilli in a small,
non-stick frying pan over medium–
high heat. Dry-fry for 1–2 minutes,
or until the chilli is dark but not burnt.
Transfer to a mortar and pestle or
spice mill, and grind until fine. Mix
the ground chilli in a bowl with the
shallots, spring onion, mint, coriander,
garlic, lime juice, palm sugar and
remaining fish sauce, stirring to
dissolve the sugar if necessary.

Cut the beef into thin strips and
place in a bowl with the dressing
and tomato. Toss well. Arrange the
lettuce on a serving platter and pile
the beef salad on top.

Serves 4

Fresh salmon patties with mango salsa

1 garlic clove, peeled
500 g fresh salmon, skin removed, roughly chopped
1 red onion, diced
50 g (½ cup) dry breadcrumbs
1 egg
50 g (1 cup) chopped coriander
1 mango, diced
60 ml (¼ cup) lime juice

Place the garlic, salmon and half the onion in a food processor and process until coarsely minced. Add the breadcrumbs, egg and half the coriander, and season. Mix together well and divide into six equal portions. Shape into patties, place on a plate, cover and refrigerate for 30 minutes. To make the salsa, place the mango, 2 tablespoons lime juice and the remaining onion and coriander in a bowl, and mix together well.

Heat a lightly greased non-stick frying pan, add the remaining lime juice and cook the patties for 4–5 minutes each side. They should be moist and slightly pink inside. To serve, place the patties on six serving plates and spoon over the salsa.

Serves 6

Note: The patties can be served between foccacia with salad greens, or with a salad and bread on the side. If unavailable, fresh salmon can be replaced by tinned salmon.

Mediterranean layered cob

2 eggplants (aubergines)
4 zucchini (courgettes)
900 g orange sweet potato
2 large red capsicums (peppers)
80 ml (1/3 cup) olive oil
23 cm round cob loaf
165 g jar pesto
200 g ricotta cheese
35 g (1/3 cup) grated Parmesan
cheese

Cut the eggplant and zucchini into
1 cm slices lengthways. Sprinkle
the eggplant with salt and drain for
30 minutes, then rinse and pat dry.

Cut the sweet potato into 5 mm
slices. Quarter the capsicums and
remove the seeds and membranes.
Grill, skin-side-up, until the skins have
blackened. Leave to cool in a plastic
bag, then remove the skins. Brush the
eggplant, sweet potato and zucchini
with olive oil and chargrill, in batches,
until lightly browned.

Cut a lid from the top of the loaf.
Remove the bread from inside, leaving
a 1 cm shell. Brush the inside of the
loaf and lid with pesto. Layer the
zucchini and capsicum inside the loaf,
then spread with the combined ricotta
and Parmesan. Layer in the sweet
potato and eggplant, lightly pressing
down to fit. Replace the lid.

Cover the loaf with plastic wrap and
place on a baking tray. Place another
tray on top and put heavy food tins
on top of the tray. Chill overnight.

Preheat the oven to 250°C (500°F/
Gas 9). Remove the plastic wrap,
return the loaf to the baking tray and
bake for about 10 minutes, or until
crispy. Cut into wedges to serve.

Serves 6

Salami pasta salad

1 red capsicum (pepper)
1 green capsicum (pepper)
4 celery stalks
1 fennel bulb, trimmed
1 red onion
200 g thickly sliced pepper-coated
  salami
15 g (½ cup) chopped flat-leaf parsley
300 g mixed coloured fettucine,
  broken into short pieces

Dressing
125 ml (½ cup) olive oil
3 tablespoons lemon juice
2½ tablespoons Dijon mustard
1 teaspoon sugar
1 garlic clove, crushed

Slice the red and green capsicums into strips and place them in a large bowl. Slice the celery and add to the bowl. Cut the fennel and onion in half, then slice and add to the bowl. Cut the salami into strips and add to the bowl along with the parsley.

Cook the fettucine in a large pan of rapidly boiling salted water until just tender. Drain and rinse in cold water. Transfer the cooked pasta to the bowl and mix thoroughly with the capsicum, celery, fennel, onion, parsley and salami.

To make the dressing, combine the olive oil, lemon juice, mustard, sugar and crushed garlic, and season to taste with salt and plenty of cracked pepper. Pour over the salad and toss well to coat.

Serves 8

Prawn skewers with coconut sambal

80 ml (1/3 cup) coconut cream
60 ml (1/4 cup) lime juice
2 tablespoons soy sauce
1 tablespoon grated lime zest
2 teaspoons chopped red chilli
1 teaspoon grated palm sugar
  or soft brown sugar
1/2 teaspoon shrimp paste
4 garlic cloves, crushed
32 raw medium prawns, peeled and
  deveined, with tails intact
2 teaspoons oil
1 tablespoon chopped coriander

mango chutney

Coconut sambal
25 g (1/4 cup) desiccated coconut
40 g (1/4 cup) sesame seeds
1/2 teaspoon dried garlic flakes
1/4 teaspoon ground coriander
1/4 teaspoon ground cumin
40 g (1/4 cup) roasted unsalted
  peanuts, roughly chopped

Soak eight bamboo skewers in water for 30 minutes.

Combine the coconut cream, lime juice, soy sauce, lime zest, chilli, sugar, shrimp paste and garlic and mix until the sugar dissolves.

Thread four prawns on each skewer. Place on a non-metallic plate and pour the marinade over them and refrigerate, covered, for 1 hour.

To make the sambal, toast the coconut in a dry frying pan for 1–2 minutes, or until golden, then add the sesame seeds, garlic flakes, spices and 1/2 teaspoon salt and cook for about 30 seconds. Remove from the heat and stir in the peanuts. Spoon into a small serving bowl.

Heat a chargrill pan or barbecue to high and brush with a little oil. Cook the prawns on both sides for 2–3 minutes, or until pink and cooked. Place on a platter and sprinkle with coriander. Serve with the sambal and chutney.

Serves 4

Roast beef and spinach salad with horseradish

200 g green beans, trimmed
500 g rump steak, cut into 3 cm
  thick pieces
1 red onion, peeled and halved
1 tablespoon olive oil
100 g (2¼ cups) baby spinach
50 g (1½ cups) watercress leaves
200 g semi-dried (sun-blushed)
  tomatoes
125 g (½ cup) plain Greek-style
  yoghurt
1 tablespoon creamed horseradish
2 tablespoons lemon juice
2 tablespoons cream
2 garlic cloves
2–3 dashes Tabasco sauce

sea salt, to taste

Bring a saucepan of water to the boil, add the beans and cook for 4 minutes, or until tender. Drain, and refresh under cold water. When cool, drain and set aside. Preheat a grill or barbecue. Brush the steak and onion with oil, and cook the steak for 2 minutes each side, or until rare. Remove the steak and leave for 5 minutes. Meanwhile, cook the onion for 2–3 minutes each side, or until charred.

Place the spinach, watercress, tomatoes and beans in a large salad bowl. In a small bowl, whisk together the yoghurt, horseradish, lemon juice, cream, garlic, Tabasco and some black pepper to taste. Chill for 15 minutes.

Slice the beef thinly across the grain, and layer carefully over the salad. Slice the grilled onion, add to the salad and drizzle with the dressing. Season well with sea salt and freshly ground black pepper.

Serves 4

Note: This cooking time will result in rare beef. Cook for a little longer if you prefer your beef medium or well done.

Caesar salad

3 eggs
3 garlic cloves, crushed
2–3 anchovy fillets
1 teaspoon Worcestershire sauce
2 tablespoons lime juice
1 teaspoon Dijon mustard
185 ml (3/4 cup) olive oil
3 slices white bread
20 g butter
1 tablespoon oil, extra
3 rashers back bacon
1 large or 4 baby cos lettuces
75 g (3/4 cup) shaved Parmesan
  cheese

Process the eggs, garlic, anchovies, Worcestershire sauce, lime juice and mustard in a food processor until smooth. With the motor running, add the oil in a thin, continuous stream to produce a creamy dressing. Season to taste with salt and freshly ground black pepper.

Cut the crusts off the bread, then cut the bread into 1.5 cm cubes. Heat the butter and extra olive oil in a frying pan over medium heat, add the bread and cook for 5–8 minutes, or until crisp, then remove from the pan. Cook the bacon in the same pan for 3 minutes, or until it is crispy, then break into bite-sized pieces.

Toss the lettuce leaves with the dressing, then stir in the croutons and bacon, and top with Parmesan.

Serves 4–6

Tequila and lime grilled prawns

32 raw large prawns
125 ml (½ cup) lime juice
60 ml (¼ cup) tequila
2 small red chillies, finely chopped
3 tablespoons chopped coriander
2 tablespoons olive oil
2 garlic cloves, crushed

Green tomato salsa
1 green tomato, seeded and diced
2 tablespoons finely chopped red onion
2 green chillies, seeded and finely diced
25 g (½ cup) chopped coriander

1 garlic clove, chopped
1 tablespoon olive oil
1 avocado
1 tablespoon lime juice

Soak eight wooden skewers in cold water for 30 minutes. Peel and devein the prawns, leaving the tails intact. Thread four prawns onto each skewer. Lay out the skewers in a single layer in a non-metallic dish.

Combine the lime juice, tequila, chilli, coriander, oil and garlic in a small jug, then pour over the prawns. Cover and marinate in the fridge for 30 minutes.

To make the salsa, mix together the tomato, onion, chilli, coriander, garlic and olive oil, then season. Cover and refrigerate until needed.

Cook the skewers on a hot lightly oiled chargrill pan or barbecue hotplate for 3–5 minutes, or until pink and cooked through, brushing with the marinade during cooking to keep the prawns moist.

Before serving, halve the avocado, remove the stone, cut the flesh into 1 cm dice, then gently mix the avocado into the salsa, stirring in the lime juice at the same time. Season to taste, then serve with the prawns.

Serves 4

Lamb, capsicum and cucumber salad

1 red onion, very thinly sliced
1 red capsicum (pepper), very thinly sliced
1 green capsicum (pepper), very thinly sliced
2 large Lebanese cucumbers, cut into batons
20 g (⅓ cup) shredded mint
3 tablespoons chopped dill
60 ml (¼ cup) olive oil
600 g lamb backstraps or fillets
80 ml (⅓ cup) lemon juice
2 small garlic cloves, crushed
100 ml extra virgin olive oil

Combine the onion, red and green capsicum, cucumber, mint and dill in a large bowl.

Heat a chargrill pan or frying pan until hot. Drizzle with the oil and cook the lamb for 2–3 minutes on each side, or until it is tender but still a little pink. Remove from the pan and allow to rest for 5 minutes. Thinly slice the lamb and add to the salad, tossing to mix.

Combine the lemon juice and garlic in a small jug, then whisk in the extra virgin olive oil with a fork until well combined. Season with salt and black pepper, then toss the dressing gently through the salad.

Serves 4

Note: This salad is delicious served on fresh or toasted Turkish bread spread with hummus.

Brown rice and puy lentils with pine nuts and spinach

200 g (1 cup) brown rice
100 ml extra virgin olive oil
1 red onion, diced
2 garlic cloves, crushed
1 carrot, diced
2 celery stalks, diced
185 g (1 cup) puy lentils (see Note)
2 tomatoes, seeded and diced
3 tablespoons chopped coriander
3 tablespoons chopped mint
2 tablespoons balsamic vinegar
1 tablespoon lemon juice
2 tablespoons toasted pine nuts
90 g (2 cups) baby spinach leaves, washed

Bring a large saucepan of water to the boil. Add 1 teaspoon salt and the rice, and cook for 20 minutes, or until tender. Drain and refresh under cold running water.

Heat 2 tablespoons oil in a saucepan and add the onion, garlic, carrot and celery. Cook over low heat for 5 minutes, or until softened, then add the puy lentils and 375 ml (1½ cups) water. Bring to the boil and simmer for 15 minutes, or until tender. Drain well, but do not rinse. Combine with the rice, tomato, coriander and mint in a large bowl.

Whisk the remaining oil with the balsamic vinegar and lemon juice, and season well with salt and freshly ground black pepper. Pour over the salad, add the pine nuts and the spinach, and toss well to combine.

Serves 6–8

Note: Puy lentils are green French lentils available at specialist food stores and some supermarkets. You can use green or brown lentils instead.

Risoni and broccoli salad with fresh herb dressing

8 garlic cloves, unpeeled
2 tablespoons extra virgin olive oil
125 g whole egg mayonnaise
100 g crème fraîche
80 g pesto
2 tablespoons lemon juice
250 g broccoli florets
400 g risoni (rice-shaped pasta)
100 g toasted slivered almonds
1 tablespoon finely chopped parsley
1 tablespoon finely chopped chives

shaved Parmesan cheese

Preheat the oven to 180°C (350°F/ Gas 4). Toss the garlic cloves in the olive oil and bake for 45 minutes, or until they are soft and golden.

Squeeze two of the garlic cloves from their skins and place in a food processor. Add the mayonnaise, crème fraîche, pesto and lemon juice, and process until just combined, then set aside until required.

Meanwhile, steam the broccoli florets for a few minutes, then refresh under cold water and drain well. Bring a large saucepan of water to the boil, then add 1 teaspoon of salt and the risoni, and cook for 8–10 minutes, or until *al dente*. Drain.

Add the almonds, dressing, parsley and chives to the risoni while still warm, and toss with the broccoli in a large bowl. Serve in deep salad bowls garnished with shaved Parmesan and a roasted garlic clove on each portion.

Serves 6

Variation: Adding some cooked, peeled king prawns will make this salad extra special.

Beef satay salad

2 teaspoons tamarind pulp
½ teaspoon sesame oil
2 tablespoons soy sauce
2 teaspoons soft brown sugar
2 garlic cloves, crushed
1 tablespoon lime juice
700 g rump steak
1 tablespoon peanut oil
6 large cos lettuce leaves, washed,
    dried and shredded
1 red capsicum (pepper), julienned
180 g (2 cups) bean sprouts
2 tablespoons fried onion flakes

Satay sauce
2 red chillies, chopped
½ teaspoon shrimp paste
1 garlic clove
6 red Asian shallots
2 teaspoons peanut oil
250 ml (1 cup) coconut milk
1 tablespoon lime juice
120 g (¾ cup) unsalted roasted
    peanuts, finely ground in a food
    processor
1 tablespoon kecap manis
1 tablespoon soft brown sugar
1 tablespoon fish sauce
2 kaffir lime leaves, shredded

Combine the tamarind pulp and 60 ml
(¼ cup) of boiling water and allow
to cool. Mash the pulp with your
fingertips to dissolve it, then strain,
reserving the liquid. Discard the pulp.

Put the sesame oil, soy sauce, sugar,
garlic, lime juice and 2 tablespoons of
tamarind water in a large bowl. Add
the steak, turn to coat, and cover with
plastic wrap. Chill for 2 hours.

Meanwhile, to make the satay sauce,
process the chillies, shrimp paste,
garlic and shallots to a paste in a
food processor. Heat the oil in a frying
pan and cook the paste for 3 minutes.
Add the coconut milk, lime juice,
ground peanuts, remaining tamarind
water, kecap manis, sugar, fish sauce
and kaffir lime leaves. Cook over
medium heat until thickened. Thin
with 125 ml (½ cup) water, and return
to the boil for 2 minutes. Season.

Heat the peanut oil in a frying pan
over high heat, and cook the steak
for 3 minutes on each side, or until
medium–rare. Leave for 3 minutes,
then thinly slice. Toss the steak slices
in a large bowl with the lettuce,
capsicum and bean sprouts. Pile onto
serving plates, drizzle with the satay
sauce, and sprinkle with the fried
onion flakes.

Serves 4

Crab salad with green mango and coconut

2 garlic cloves, peeled
2 small red chillies
2 tablespoons dried shrimp
2 tablespoons fish sauce
3 tablespoons lime juice
3 teaspoons palm sugar or soft
  brown sugar
30 g (½ cup) shredded coconut
  (see Notes)
300 g (1½ cups) shredded green
  mango
10 g (½ cup) mint leaves (torn if
  very big)
15 g (½ cup) coriander leaves
3 kaffir lime leaves, shredded
2 teaspoons thinly shredded, pickled
  ginger
500 g fresh crabmeat

banana leaves, optional
crushed toasted peanuts
lime wedges

Preheat the oven to 180°C (350°F/ Gas 4). Place the garlic, chillies, dried shrimp and ½ teaspoon salt in a mortar and pestle. Pound to a paste, then whisk in the fish sauce, lime juice and palm sugar with a fork.

Place the shredded coconut on a baking tray and bake for 3–5 minutes, shaking the tray occasionally to ensure even toasting. Watch the coconut closely, as it will burn easily.

Place the shredded mango in a large bowl and add the mint, coriander, kaffir lime leaves, ginger, coconut and crabmeat. Pour on the dressing and toss together gently.

Place a piece of banana leaf (if using) in each serving bowl. Mound some crab salad on top, sprinkle with the peanuts and serve immediately with lime wedges.

Serves 4–6

Notes: Freshly shredded coconut is delicious, so if you have the time, remove the skin from a coconut and shred using a vegetable peeler. The banana leaves are for presentation only, and are not edible.

Spicy lamb and noodle salad

1 tablespoon five-spice powder
60 ml (¼ cup) vegetable oil
2 garlic cloves, crushed
2 lamb backstraps or fillets (about 250 g each)
500 g fresh Shanghai (wheat) noodles
1½ teaspoons sesame oil
80 g snow pea (mangetout) sprouts
½ red capsicum (pepper), thinly sliced
4 spring onions, thinly sliced on the diagonal
2 tablespoons sesame seeds, toasted

Dressing
1 tablespoon finely chopped fresh ginger
1 tablespoon Chinese black vinegar
1 tablespoon Chinese rice wine
2 tablespoons peanut oil
2 teaspoons chilli oil

Combine the five-spice powder, 2 tablespoons of the vegetable oil and garlic in a large bowl. Add the lamb and turn to coat well. Cover and marinate for 30 minutes.

Cook the noodles in a large saucepan of boiling water for 4–5 minutes, or until tender. Drain, rinse with cold water and drain again. Add the sesame oil and toss to combine.

Heat the remaining vegetable oil in a large frying pan. Cook the lamb over medium–high heat for 3 minutes each side for medium–rare, or until cooked to your liking. Rest for 5 minutes, then thinly slice across the grain.

To make the dressing, combine the ginger, Chinese black vinegar, rice wine, peanut oil and chilli oil.

Place the noodles, lamb strips, snow pea sprouts, capsicum, spring onion and the dressing in a large bowl and toss gently until well combined. Sprinkle with the sesame seeds and serve immediately.

Serves 4

Crab, Camembert and fusilli frittata

80 g tri-coloured fusilli
1 tablespoon olive oil
1 very small red onion, finely chopped
1 large Roma (plum) tomato, roughly chopped
60 g (⅓ cup) semi-dried (sun-blushed) tomatoes, roughly chopped
2 tablespoons finely chopped coriander leaves
140 g (⅔ cup) cooked fresh or tinned crab meat
150 g Camembert cheese, rind removed, cut into small pieces
6 eggs plus 2 egg yolks

Cook the pasta in a large saucepan of boiling water until *al dente*. Drain, rinse, then drain again and set aside to cool. Meanwhile, heat half the oil in a small frying pan over low heat, add the onion and cook for 4–5 minutes, or until softened but not browned. Transfer to a bowl and add the Roma tomato, semi-dried tomatoes and coriander. Squeeze out any excess moisture from the crab meat and add the meat to the bowl. Add half the cheese to the bowl, then add the cooled pasta. Mix well. Beat together the six eggs and the two extra yolks, then stir into the tomato and crab mixture. Season.

Heat the remaining oil in the frying pan, pour in the frittata mixture and cook over low heat for 25 minutes. Preheat the grill to low. Scatter the remaining Camembert over the frittata before placing it under the grill for 10–15 minutes, or until cooked and golden brown on top. Remove from the grill and leave for 5 minutes. Cut into slices and serve with salad and some bread.

Serves 4–6

Asian tofu salad

1 large red capsicum (pepper)
1 large green capsicum (pepper)
180 g (2 cups) bean sprouts
4 spring onions, sliced diagonally
15 g (¼ cup) chopped coriander
450 g (3 cups) shredded Chinese
  cabbage
40 g (¼ cup) chopped roasted
  peanuts
450 g firm tofu
60 ml (¼ cup) peanut oil

Dressing
2 tablespoons sweet chilli sauce
2 tablespoons lime juice
½ teaspoon sesame oil
1½ tablespoons light soy sauce
1 garlic clove, finely chopped
3 teaspoons finely grated fresh ginger
60 ml (¼ cup) peanut oil

Thinly slice the capsicums, and combine with the bean sprouts, spring onion, coriander, cabbage and peanuts.

Drain the liquid from the tofu and cut into 8 x 2 cm wide slices. Heat the oil in a large, frying pan. Cook the tofu for 2–3 minutes on each side, or until it is golden with a crispy edge, and add to the salad.

To make the dressing, mix together the chilli sauce, lime juice, oil, soy, garlic and ginger. Whisk in the peanut oil, then toss through the salad and serve immediately.

Serves 4–6

Prawn and rice noodle salad

250 g rice stick noodles
700 g medium cooked prawns,
  peeled and deveined, with tails
  intact
1 carrot, coarsely grated
1 small Lebanese cucumber, thinly
  sliced
30 g (1 cup) coriander leaves
80 g (½ cup) roasted unsalted
  peanuts, chopped
50 g (¼ cup) crisp fried shallots
  (see Note)

Dressing
125 ml (½ cup) rice vinegar
1 tablespoon grated palm sugar
  or soft brown sugar
1 garlic clove, finely chopped
2 red chillies, finely chopped
60 ml (¼ cup) fish sauce
60 ml (¼ cup) lime juice
2 tablespoons peanut oil

Soak the noodles in boiling water in a large heatproof bowl for 10 minutes. Drain, rinse under cold water to cool, and drain again. Place in a large serving bowl.

Add the prawns, carrot, cucumber and coriander to the bowl and toss.

To make the dressing, combine the vinegar, sugar and garlic in a small saucepan and bring to the boil, then reduce the heat and simmer for 3 minutes to slightly reduce the liquid. Transfer to a bowl and add the chilli, fish sauce and lime juice. Slowly whisk in the oil, and season to taste.

Toss the dressing through the salad, then scatter with the peanuts and crisp fried shallots and serve.

Serves 4

Note: Crisp fried shallots are red Asian shallot flakes used as a garnish in Southeast Asia. They are available from Asian food stores.

Chargrilled vegetable terrine

8 large slices chargrilled eggplant
(aubergine), drained
10 slices chargrilled red capsicum
(pepper), drained
8 slices chargrilled zucchini
(courgette), drained
350 g ricotta cheese
2 garlic cloves, crushed
45 g rocket
3 marinated artichokes, drained and
sliced
85 g semi-dried (sun-blushed)
tomatoes, drained and chopped
100 g marinated mushrooms, drained
and halved

Line a 23.5 x 13 x 6.5 cm loaf tin
with plastic wrap, leaving a generous
overhang on each side. Line the base
with half the eggplant, cutting to fit.
Next layer in half the capsicum, then
all of the zucchini.

Beat the ricotta and garlic together
until smooth. Season, then spread
evenly over the zucchini. Press down
firmly, and top with the rocket leaves.
Arrange the marinated artichoke,
tomato and mushrooms in three
strips over the rocket.

Top with another layer of capsicum
and finish with the eggplant. Cover
securely with the overhanging plastic
wrap. Top with a piece of cardboard
and weigh it down. Chill overnight.

Peel back the plastic wrap and
carefully turn out the terrine onto
a plate. Remove the plastic wrap
and cut into thick slices to serve.

Serves 8

Wild rice and roast chicken with Asian dressing

190 g (1 cup) wild rice
200 g (1 cup) jasmine rice
1 Chinese barbecue roast chicken
  (see Note)
15 g (¼ cup) chopped mint
15 g (¼ cup) chopped coriander
1 large Lebanese cucumber
6 spring onions
80 g (½ cup) roasted peanuts,
  roughly chopped
80 ml (⅓ cup) mirin
2 tablespoons Chinese rice wine
1 tablespoon soy sauce
1 tablespoon lime juice
2 tablespoons sweet chilli sauce,
  plus extra, to serve

Bring a large saucepan of water to the boil and add 1 teaspoon of salt and the wild rice. Cook for 30 minutes, add the jasmine rice and cook for a further 10 minutes, or until tender. Drain the rice, refresh under cold water and drain again.

Shred the chicken (the skin as well) into bite-sized pieces, place in a large bowl and add the mint and coriander. Cut the cucumber through the centre (do not peel) and slice thinly on the diagonal. Slice the spring onions on the diagonal. Add the cucumber, spring onion, rice and peanuts to the bowl with the chicken.

Mix together the mirin, rice wine, soy, lime juice and sweet chilli sauce in a small jug, pour over the salad and toss to combine. Pile the salad onto serving platters and serve with extra chilli sauce.

Serves 8

Note: It is important to use a Chinese barbecued chicken, available from Chinese barbecue shops. The flavours of five-spice and soy used to cook it will add to the flavour of the dish.

Modern salad Niçoise

60 ml (¼ cup) lemon juice
1 garlic clove, crushed
140 ml olive oil
400 g waxy potatoes, such as
  Charlotte or Kipfler
3 eggs
120 g green beans, trimmed
1 green capsicum (pepper), seeded
  and sliced
120 g black olives
300 g firm, ripe tomatoes, cut into
  wedges
100 g cucumber, cut into chunks
3 spring onions, cut into 2 cm pieces
600 g fresh tuna steaks

Place the lemon juice, garlic and 120 ml of olive oil in a jar with a screw-top lid. Season and shake the jar well to combine.

Boil the potatoes in a saucepan of salted water, for 10–12 minutes, or until tender. Add the eggs for the final 8 minutes of cooking. Drain, cool the eggs under cold water, then peel and quarter. Cool the potatoes, then cut into chunks. Bring a saucepan of salted water to the boil, add the green beans and blanch for 3 minutes. Drain and refresh under cold water. Drain well, then slice in half on the diagonal.

Place the potato and beans in a large bowl, and add the capsicum, olives, tomatoes, cucumber and spring onion. Strain the garlic from the dressing, then shake again so it is combined. Pour half over the salad, toss and transfer to a serving dish.

Heat a frying pan over very high heat. Add the remaining olive oil and allow to heat. Season the tuna steaks well on both sides and cook for 2 minutes on each side, or until rare. Allow the tuna to cool for 5 minutes, then slice thinly. Arrange on top of the salad with the eggs, and drizzle with the remaining dressing.

Serves 4

Asian pork salad

2 teaspoons rice vinegar
1 small red chilli, finely chopped
2 tablespoons light soy sauce
1 teaspoon julienned fresh ginger
¼ teaspoon sesame oil
1 star anise
2 teaspoons lime juice
250 g Chinese roasted pork (char siu)
100 g snow pea (mangetout) sprouts
2 spring onions, thinly sliced on the
    diagonal
½ red capsicum (pepper), thinly sliced

For the dressing, combine the vinegar, chilli, soy sauce, ginger, sesame oil, star anise and lime juice in a small saucepan. Gently warm for 2 minutes, or until just about to come to the boil, then set aside to cool. Once it is cool, remove the star anise.

Thinly slice the pork and place in a serving bowl. Pick over the sprouts, discarding any brown or broken ones, and add to the pork. Add the spring onion and capsicum, pour on the dressing, and toss well.

Serves 4

Prawn and bean salad

200 g (1 cup) dried cannellini beans
2 red capsicums (peppers), cut into
　large flattish pieces
300 g green beans, trimmed
150 g (½ loaf) day-old ciabatta bread
　or other crusty loaf
80 ml (⅓ cup) olive oil
1 large garlic clove, finely chopped
1 kg raw medium prawns, peeled and
　deveined, with tails intact
30 g (1½ cups) flat-leaf parsley

Dressing
60 ml (¼ cup) lemon juice
60 ml (¼ cup) olive oil
2 tablespoons capers, rinsed,
　drained and chopped
1 teaspoon sugar, optional

Soak the cannellini beans in a large
bowl of cold water for 8 hours. Drain
then rinse the beans well, transfer to
a saucepan, cover with cold water
and cook for 20–30 minutes, or until
tender. Drain, rinse under cold water,
drain again and put in a serving bowl.

Cook the capsicum, skin-side-up,
under a hot grill until the skin blackens
and blisters. Cool in a plastic bag,
then peel. Cut into strips, and add
to the bowl.

Cook the green beans in a saucepan
of boiling water for 3–4 minutes, or
until tender. Drain and add to the
serving bowl. Cut the bread into six
slices, then cut each slice in four.
Heat 60 ml (¼ cup) of the oil in a
frying pan and cook the bread over
medium heat on each side until
golden. Remove from the pan.

Heat the remaining oil in the frying
pan, add the garlic and prawns and
cook for 1–2 minutes, or until the
prawns are pink and cooked. Add
to the salad with the parsley.

Combine the dressing ingredients,
then season. Toss the dressing and
bread through the salad.

Serves 4

Marinated grilled tofu salad with ginger miso dressing

80 ml (⅓ cup) tamari, shoyu or light
  soy sauce
2 teaspoons oil
2 garlic cloves, crushed
1 teaspoon grated fresh ginger
1 teaspoon chilli paste
500 g firm tofu, cut into 2 cm cubes
400 g mixed salad leaves
1 Lebanese cucumber, finely sliced
250 g cherry tomatoes, halved
2 teaspoons oil, extra

Dressing
2 teaspoons white miso paste
2 tablespoons mirin
1 teaspoon sesame oil
1 teaspoon grated fresh ginger
1 teaspoon finely chopped chives
1 tablespoon toasted sesame seeds

Mix together the tamari, oil, garlic, ginger, chilli paste and ½ teaspoon salt in a bowl. Add the tofu and mix until well coated. Marinate for at least 10 minutes, or preferably overnight. Drain and reserve the marinade.

To make the dressing, combine the miso with 125 ml (½ cup) hot water and leave until the miso dissolves. Add the mirin, sesame oil, ginger, chives and sesame seeds and stir thoroughly until it begins to thicken.

Combine the mesclun leaves, cucumber and tomato in a serving bowl and leave until ready to serve.

Heat the extra oil on a chargrill. Add the tofu and cook over medium heat for 4 minutes, or until golden brown. Pour on the reserved marinade and cook for 1 minute over high heat. Remove from the grill and allow to cool for 5 minutes.

Add the tofu to the salad, drizzle with the dressing and toss well.

Serves 4

Note: Miso is Japanese bean paste and plays an important part in their cuisine. It is commonly used in soups, dressings, on grilled foods and as a flavouring for pickles.

Chicken and tzatziki wrap

½ telegraph cucumber, seeded and
  grated
100 g low-fat natural yoghurt
¼ teaspoon lemon juice
1 tablespoon chopped mint
4 skinless chicken thigh fillets
pinch paprika
4 sheets lavash or other flat bread
  (see Note)
4 large butter lettuce leaves

Sprinkle the grated cucumber with
½ teaspoon salt. Leave the cucumber
for 10 minutes, then drain and mix
with the yoghurt, lemon juice and
mint. Season.

Flatten the chicken thigh fillets with
a meat mallet or rolling pin, season
and sprinkle with the paprika. Grill
the fillets for 5–7 minutes on each
side, or until cooked through.

Lay out the lavash breads and place
a large butter lettuce leaf on each.
Spread each with one quarter of the
tzatziki, then top with a sliced chicken
fillet. Roll up, folding one end closed.
Wrap in baking paper to serve.

Makes 4

Note: If you can't find lavash, use any
thin, flat bread that will roll up easily.

Pepper-crusted salmon salad

1 tablespoon coarsely ground black
  pepper
4 salmon fillets (approximately 180 g
  each), skin removed
80 g (⅓ cup) mayonnaise
1½ tablespoons lemon juice
2 teaspoons creamed horseradish
1 small garlic clove, crushed
2 tablespoons chopped parsley
100 g watercress
3 tablespoons olive oil
25 g butter
100 g butter lettuce

Mix the pepper and ¼ teaspoon salt together in a bowl, and coat both sides of each salmon fillet, pressing the pepper down firmly with your fingers. Chill for 30 minutes.

Blend the mayonnaise, lemon juice, horseradish, garlic, parsley, 60 g of the watercress, 1 tablespoon of oil and 1 tablespoon of warm water in a food processor for 1 minute. Chill.

Heat the butter and 1 tablespoon oil in a large frying pan until bubbling. Add the salmon fillets and cook over medium–high heat for 2–3 minutes each side, or until cooked to your liking. Remove from the pan and allow to cool slightly.

Wash and dry the butter lettuce, and tear into small pieces. Arrange the lettuce and remaining watercress in the centre of four serving plates, and drizzle lightly with the remaining olive oil. Break each salmon fillet into four or five pieces and arrange over the lettuce. Pour the dressing over the salmon and in a circle around the outside of the leaves.

Serves 4

Roasted tomato and pasta salad with pesto

140 ml olive oil
500 g cherry tomatoes
5 garlic cloves, unpeeled
400 g penne pasta
90 g (1/3 cup) pesto
3 tablespoons balsamic vinegar

basil leaves

Preheat the oven to 180°C (350°F/ Gas 4). Place 2 tablespoons of oil in a roasting dish and place in the hot oven for 5 minutes. Add the tomatoes and garlic to the dish, season well and toss until the tomatoes are well coated. Return to the oven and roast for 30 minutes.

Meanwhile, cook the pasta in a large saucepan of rapidly boiling water until *al dente*. Drain and transfer to a large serving bowl.

Squeeze the flesh from the roasted garlic cloves into a bowl. Add the remaining olive oil, the pesto, vinegar and 3 tablespoons of the tomato cooking juices. Season with a little salt and pepper, and toss to combine. Add to the pasta and mix well, ensuring that the pasta is coated in the dressing. Gently stir in the cherry tomatoes, then scatter with basil. This salad can be prepared up to 4 hours ahead, and served warm or cold.

Serves 4

Beef teriyaki with cucumber salad

80 ml (⅓ cup) soy sauce
2 tablespoons mirin
1 tablespoon sake (optional)
1 garlic clove, crushed
1 teaspoon grated fresh ginger
4 fillet steaks
1 teaspoon sugar
1 teaspoon toasted sesame seeds

Cucumber salad
1 large Lebanese cucumber, peeled, seeded and diced
½ red capsicum (pepper), diced
2 spring onions, sliced thinly on the diagonal
2 teaspoons sugar
1 tablespoon rice wine vinegar

Combine the soy, mirin, sake, garlic and ginger and pour over the steaks. Cover with plastic wrap and chill for at least 30 minutes.

To make the cucumber salad, place the cucumber, capsicum and spring onion in a bowl. Place the sugar, rice wine vinegar and 60 ml (¼ cup) water in a saucepan and stir over medium heat until the sugar dissolves. Increase the heat and simmer for 3–4 minutes, or until thickened. Pour over the cucumber salad, stir to combine and leave to cool completely.

Spray a chargrill plate with oil spray and heat until very hot. Drain the steaks and reserve the marinade. Cook for 3–4 minutes on each side, or until cooked to your liking. Rest the meat for 5–10 minutes.

Place the sugar and the reserved marinade in a saucepan and heat, stirring, until the sugar has dissolved. Bring to the boil and simmer for 2 minutes. Keep warm.

Slice each steak into 1 cm strips and arrange a steak on each plate. Spoon on some of the marinade, some salad and garnish with sesame seeds. Serve with steamed rice and the remaining cucumber salad.

Serves 4

Tofu kebabs with coriander miso

1 large red capsicum (pepper), cut into squares
12 button mushrooms, halved
6 pickling onions, quartered
3 zucchini (courgettes), cut into 3 cm chunks
450 g firm tofu, cut into 2 cm cubes
125 ml (½ cup) light olive oil
60 ml (¼ cup) light soy sauce
2 garlic cloves, crushed
2 teaspoons grated fresh ginger

Coriander miso
80 g (½ cup) unsalted roasted peanuts
60 g (2 cups) firmly packed coriander leaves
2 tablespoons white miso paste
2 garlic cloves
100 ml olive oil

Soak 12 wooden skewers in cold water for 10 minutes. Thread the vegetable pieces and tofu alternately onto the skewers, then place in a large rectangular ceramic dish.

Combine the olive oil, soy sauce, garlic and ginger in a bowl, then pour half the mixture over the kebabs. Cover with plastic wrap and marinate for 1 hour.

To make the miso pesto, finely chop the peanuts, coriander leaves, miso paste and garlic in a food processor. Slowly add the olive oil while the machine is still running and blend until a smooth paste.

Heat a grill plate and cook the kebabs, turning and brushing frequently with the remaining marinade, for 4–6 minutes, or until the edges are slightly brown. Serve with steamed rice and a little of the miso pesto.

Serves 4

Chilli chicken and cashew salad

3 tablespoons sweet chilli sauce
2 tablespoons lime juice
2 teaspoons fish sauce
2 tablespoons chopped coriander
1 garlic clove, crushed
1 small red chilli, finely chopped
1½ teaspoons grated fresh ginger
2 tablespoons olive oil
600 g chicken breast fillets
100 g salad leaves
250 g cherry tomatoes, halved
100 g Lebanese cucumber, cut into
 bite-sized chunks
50 g snow pea (mangetout) sprouts,
 trimmed
80 g (½ cup) cashew nuts, roughly
 chopped

Combine the chilli sauce, lime juice, fish sauce, coriander, garlic, chilli, ginger and 1 tablespoon of the oil in a large bowl.

Heat the remaining oil in a frying or chargrill pan over medium heat until hot, and cook the chicken for 5–8 minutes on each side or until cooked through. While still hot, slice each breast widthways into 1 cm slices and toss in the bowl with the dressing. Leave to cool slightly.

Combine the salad leaves, cherry tomatoes, cucumber chunks and snow pea sprouts in a serving bowl. Add the chicken and all of the dressing, and toss gently until the leaves are lightly coated. Scatter with chopped cashews and serve.

Serves 4

Squid salad with salsa verde

800 g small–medium squid, cleaned,
   scored and sliced into 4 cm
   diamonds
2 tablespoons olive oil
2 tablespoons lime juice
150 g green beans
150 g asparagus spears
1 teaspoon oil, extra
100 g baby rocket

Salsa verde
1 thick slice white bread, crusts
   removed
140 ml olive oil
3 tablespoons finely chopped parsley
2 teaspoons finely grated lemon zest
60 ml (¼ cup) lemon juice
2 anchovy fillets, finely chopped
2 tablespoons capers, rinsed and
   drained
1 garlic clove, crushed

Combine the squid pieces in a bowl with the olive oil, lime juice, and a little salt and pepper, then cover with plastic wrap and place in the refrigerator to marinate for 2 hours.

To make the salsa verde, break the bread into chunks and drizzle with 2 tablespoons of oil, mixing with your hands so that the oil is absorbed. Place the bread and remaining oil in a food processor with the remaining salsa ingredients, and blend to a paste. If it is too thick, thin with lemon juice and olive oil, to taste.

Trim the green beans and asparagus, and cut in half on the diagonal. Blanch the beans for 3 minutes, refresh under cold water, then drain. Blanch the asparagus for 1–2 minutes, refresh in cold water then drain.

Heat the extra oil in a frying pan over high heat, and cook the marinated squid in batches for 3 minutes per batch or until cooked. Cool slightly.

Combine the green beans, asparagus, rocket and squid. Add 3 tablespoons of the salsa verde and toss gently. Arrange on a serving platter and drizzle with another tablespoon of salsa verde.

Serves 4

Piri piri prawns

1 kg raw large prawns
4 long red chillies, deseeded
185 ml (¾ cup) white wine vinegar
2 large garlic cloves, chopped
6–8 small red chillies, chopped
125 ml (½ cup) olive oil
150 g mixed lettuce leaves

Remove the heads from the prawns. Slice the prawns down the back without cutting right through, leaving the tail intact. Open the prawn out and remove the vein. Place the prawns in a non-metallic bowl, cover and refrigerate until needed.

Place the long chillies in a saucepan with the vinegar and simmer over medium–high heat for 5 minutes, or until the chillies are soft. Cool slightly. Transfer the chillies and 60 ml (¼ cup) of the vinegar to a food processor (reserve the rest of the vinegar), then add the garlic and chopped chilli and blend until smooth.

With the motor running, gradually add the oil and remaining vinegar and process until well combined. Coat the prawns in the sauce, then cover and chill for 30 minutes.

Heat a chargrill pan or barbecue to high. Oil the pan, then cook the prawns, basting with the marinade, for 2–3 minutes each side, or until cooked. Boil the remaining marinade in a small saucepan, then reduce the heat and simmer for 3–4 minutes, or until slightly thickened and reduced. Divide the lettuce among four plates and arrange the prawns on top. Serve immediately with the remaining sauce.

Serves 4

Tofu fajitas

4 tablespoons light soy sauce
2 garlic cloves, crushed
400 g smoked tofu, cut into 5 cm
   strips
200 g tinned tomatoes
1 small onion, roughly chopped
1 small red chilli, seeded and finely
   chopped
3 tablespoons chopped coriander
   leaves
1 large ripe avocado
2 teaspoons lemon juice
250 g (1 cup) sour cream
2 tablespoons oil
1 red capsicum (pepper), seeded
   and sliced
1 yellow capsicum (pepper), seeded
   and sliced
8 spring onions, cut into 5 cm lengths
8 large (15 cm) flour tortillas

Place the soy sauce, garlic and 1 teaspoon pepper in a shallow dish. Add the tofu and toss together well. Cover and leave to marinate.

Combine the tomatoes, onion, chilli and coriander in a food processor until smooth. Season with salt and pepper. Transfer to a small saucepan, and bring to the boil. Reduce the heat and simmer for 10 minutes. Cool.

Halve the avocado and remove the stone. Scoop out the flesh and add the lemon juice and 2 tablespoons of the sour cream. Season and mash well with a fork.

Heat 1 tablespoon oil in a frying pan. Add the tofu and remaining marinade and cook, stirring, over high heat for 4–5 minutes. Remove from the pan. Heat the remaining oil in the pan. Add the capsicum and spring onion, season and cook for 3–4 minutes.

Dry-fry the tortillas over high heat for 5 seconds on each side.

To serve, spread a tortilla with a little avocado mixture, tomato salsa and sour cream. Top with some tofu and vegetables, fold in one end and roll. Repeat with the remaining tortillas and fillings.

Serves 4

Sesame-coated tuna with coriander salsa

4 tuna steaks
115 g (³/₄ cup) sesame seeds
olive oil for shallow-frying
100 g baby rocket

Coriander salsa
2 tomatoes, seeded and diced
1 large garlic clove, crushed
2 tablespoons finely chopped
   coriander leaves
2 tablespoons virgin olive oil
1 tablespoon lime juice

chilli jam, optional

Cut each tuna steak into three pieces. Place the sesame seeds on a sheet of baking paper. Roll the tuna in the sesame seeds to coat. Refrigerate for 15 minutes.

To make the salsa, place the tomato, garlic, coriander, oil and lime juice in a bowl, and mix together well. Cover and refrigerate until ready to use.

Fill a heavy-based frying pan to 1.5 cm with the oil and place over high heat. Add the tuna in two batches and cook for 2 minutes each side (it should be pink in the centre). Remove and drain on paper towels. To serve, divide the rocket among four serving plates and arrange the tuna over the top. Spoon the salsa on the side and serve immediately. Top with a teaspoon of chilli jam, if desired, and season.

Serves 4

Warm minted chicken and pasta salad

250 g cotelli pasta
125 ml (½ cup) olive oil
1 large red capsicum (pepper)
3 chicken breast fillets
6 spring onions, cut into 2 cm lengths
4 garlic cloves, thinly sliced
35 g (¾ cup) chopped mint
80 ml (⅓ cup) cider vinegar
100 g baby English spinach leaves

Cook the pasta in a large saucepan of boiling water until *al dente*, drain, stir in 1 tablespoon of the oil and set aside. Meanwhile, cut the capsicum into quarters, removing the seeds and membrane. Place, skin-side-up, under a hot grill for 8–10 minutes, or until the skin blackens and blisters. Cool in a plastic bag, then peel away the skin. Cut into thin strips. Place the chicken between two sheets of plastic wrap and press with the palm of your hand until slightly flattened.

Heat 1 tablespoon of the oil in a large frying pan, add the chicken and cook over medium heat for 2–3 minutes each side, or until light brown and cooked through. Remove from the pan and cut into 5 mm slices.

Add another tablespoon of the oil to the pan and add the spring onion, sliced garlic and capsicum and cook, stirring, for 2–3 minutes, or until starting to soften. Add 25 g (½ cup) of the mint, the vinegar and the remaining oil and stir until warmed through. In a large bowl, combine the pasta, chicken, spinach, onion mixture and remaining mint and toss well, seasoning to taste. Serve warm.

Serves 4

Pork and veal terrine

8–10 thin slices rindless streaky
  bacon
1 tablespoon olive oil
1 onion, chopped
2 garlic cloves, crushed
1 kg minced pork and veal
80 g (1 cup) fresh breadcrumbs
1 egg, beaten
60 ml (¼ cup) brandy
3 teaspoons chopped thyme
15 g (¼ cup) chopped parsley

Preheat the oven to 180°C (350°F/
Gas 4). Lightly grease a 25 x 11 cm
terrine. Line the terrine with the bacon
so that it hangs over the sides.

Heat the oil in a frying pan, add
the onion and garlic and cook for
2–3 minutes, or until the onion is
soft. Mix the onion with the mince,
breadcrumbs, egg, brandy, thyme
and parsley in a large bowl. Season.
Fry a piece of the mixture to check
the seasoning, and adjust if necessary.

Spoon the mixture into the lined
terrine, pressing down firmly. Fold
the bacon over the top, cover with
foil and place in a baking dish.

Place enough cold water in the baking
dish to come half-way up the side of
the terrine. Bake for 1–1¼ hours, or
until the juices run clear when the
terrine is pierced with a skewer.
Remove the terrine from the water-
filled baking dish and pour off the
excess juices. Cover with foil, then
put a piece of heavy cardboard,
cut to fit, on top of the terrine. Put
weights or food tins on top of the
cardboard to compress the terrine.
Refrigerate overnight, then cut into
slices to serve.

Serves 6

Roast duck salad with chilli dressing

½ teaspoon chilli flakes
2½ tablespoons fish sauce
1 tablespoon lime juice
2 teaspoons grated palm sugar
1 Chinese roasted duck
1 small red onion, thinly sliced
1 tablespoon julienned fresh ginger
20 g (⅓ cup) roughly chopped
  coriander
20 g (⅓ cup) roughly chopped mint
80 g (½ cup) roasted cashews
90 g butter lettuce

Place the chilli flakes in a frying pan and dry-fry for 30 seconds, then grind to a powder in a mortar and pestle or spice grinder. Combine the chilli with the fish sauce, lime juice and palm sugar in a bowl, and set aside.

Remove the flesh from the duck and cut it into bite-sized pieces. Place the duck in a bowl with the onion, ginger, coriander, mint and cashews. Pour in the dressing and toss gently.

Place the lettuce on a serving platter. Top with the duck salad and serve.

Serves 4–6

Seafood salad

500 g small squid
1 kg large clams
1 kg black mussels
500 g raw medium prawns, peeled,
    deveined, tails intact
5 tablespoons finely chopped flat-leaf
    parsley

Dressing
2 tablespoons lemon juice
80 ml (⅓ cup) olive oil
1 garlic clove, crushed

Gently pull apart the body and tentacles of the squid to separate. Remove the head by cutting below the eyes. Push out the beak and discard. Pull the quill from the body of the squid and discard. Under cold running water, pull away all the skin (the flaps can be used). Rinse well, then slice the squid into rings.

Scrub the clams and mussels and remove the beards. Discard any that are cracked or don't close when tapped. Rinse under running water. Fill a saucepan with 2 cm water, add the clams and mussels, cover, and boil for 4–5 minutes, or until the shells open. Remove, reserving the liquid. Discard any that do not open. Remove the mussels and clams from their shells and place in a bowl.

Bring 1 litre water to the boil and add the prawns and squid. Cook for 3–4 minutes, or until the prawns turn pink and the squid is tender. Drain and add to the clams and mussels.

To make the dressing, whisk all of the ingredients together. Season. Pour over the seafood, add 4 tablespoons of the parsley and toss to coat. Cover and refrigerate for 30–40 minutes. Sprinkle with the remaining parsley and serve with fresh bread.

Serves 4

Penne with prawns

3 Roma (plum) tomatoes
375 g penne pasta
500 g cooked medium prawns
100 g baby English spinach leaves
125 g goat's cheese, crumbled
40 g (¼ cup) pine nuts, toasted

Garlic dressing
2 garlic cloves, crushed
60 ml (¼ cup) extra virgin olive oil
2 teaspoons finely grated lemon zest
2 tablespoons lemon juice
1 tablespoon chopped flat-leaf
  parsley

Preheat the oven to 180°C (350°F/ Gas 4). Cut each Roma tomato lengthways into six wedges and bake on a baking tray lined with baking paper for 45 minutes, or until the wedges are just starting to dry out around the edges. Remove and cool.

Cook the penne in a large saucepan of rapidly boiling salted water for 12 minutes, or until *al dente*. Drain and cool. Transfer to a large bowl.

Meanwhile, peel the prawns, leaving the tails intact. Gently pull out the dark vein from each prawn back, starting at the head end.

Add the cooled tomato, prawns, spinach and cheese to the pasta and toss well.

For the garlic dressing, place all the ingredients in a screw-top jar, screw the lid on tightly and shake well. Pour over the salad and toss until well distributed. Sprinkle with pine nuts and serve.

Serves 4

Thai marinated octopus salad

8 baby octopus or 4 large octopus,
  cut in half (about 380 g)
250 ml (1 cup) sweet chilli sauce
2 tablespoons lime juice
1 stalk lemon grass, trimmed and
  finely chopped
2 Lebanese cucumbers
50 g butter lettuce, torn into rough
  pieces
50 g (1 cup) coriander, with stalks

Using a small knife, carefully cut between the head and tentacles of the octopus, just below the eyes. Grasp the body of the octopus and push the beak out with your finger. Cut the eyes from the head of the octopus and discard the eye section. Carefully slit through one side, avoiding the ink sac, and scrape out the gut. Rinse under running water to remove any remaining gut.

Put the octopus in a bowl and add the chilli sauce, lime juice and lemon grass. Stir until well mixed. Cover with plastic wrap and chill for at least 4 hours.

Cut the cucumbers into 6 cm lengths, scoop out the seeds and discard. Cut the cucumbers into batons.

Heat a chargrill pan until hot. Remove the octopus from the marinade, reserving the marinade, and cook for 2–3 minutes or until cooked through. Cool slightly. Arrange the lettuce and coriander around the edge of a plate, and pile the octopus in the centre.

Add the remaining marinade to the chargrill pan and heat gently for 2 minutes. Toss the cucumber through the marinade to warm, then spoon over the salad.

Serves 4

Miso yakitori chicken

3 tablespoons yellow or red miso
  paste
2 tablespoons sugar
60 ml (¼ cup) sake
2 tablespoons mirin
1 kg chicken thighs, boned (skin on)
1 cucumber
2 spring onions, cut into 2 cm pieces

Soak 12 long wooden bamboo skewers in cold water for at least 10 minutes. Place the miso, sugar, sake and mirin in a small saucepan over medium heat and cook, stirring well, for 2 minutes, or until the sauce is smooth and the sugar has dissolved completely.

Cut the chicken into 2.5 cm cubes. Seed the cucumber and cut into 2 cm batons. Thread the chicken, cucumber and spring onion pieces alternately onto the skewers — you should have three pieces of chicken, three pieces of cucumber and three pieces of spring onion per skewer.

Cook on a chargrill plate over high heat, turning occasionally, for 10 minutes, or until the chicken is almost cooked. Brush with the miso sauce and continue cooking, then turn and brush the other side. Repeat this process once or twice until the chicken and vegetables are cooked. Serve immediately with rice and salad.

Serves 4

Squid and scallops with herb dressing

2 oranges
8 small squid
200 g scallops, without roe
2 tablespoons oil
150 g rocket
3 ripe Roma (plum) tomatoes,
  chopped

Herb dressing
50 g (1 cup) finely chopped coriander
30 g (1 cup) finely chopped flat-leaf
  parsley
2 teaspoons ground cumin
1 teaspoon paprika
60 ml (1/4 cup) lime juice
60 ml (1/4 cup) olive oil

Remove the skin and white pith from the oranges. Use a sharp knife to cut between the membranes and divide into segments. Remove the seeds.

To clean the squid, gently pull the tentacles away from the tubes. Remove the intestines from the tentacles by cutting under the eyes, then push out the beaks. Pull the quill from the tubes. Peel off the skin under cold running water. Wash the tubes and tentacles and place in a bowl of water with 1/4 teaspoon salt and mix. Cover and chill for about 30 minutes. Drain and cut the tubes into long strips and the tentacles into pieces.

Pull any membrane, vein or hard white muscle from the scallops. Rinse and pat dry.

Heat the oil in a large deep frying pan over high heat and cook the squid in batches for 1–2 minutes, or until it turns white. Do not overcook or it will be tough. Drain on paper towels. Add the scallops to the pan and cook for 1–2 minutes each side, or until tender.

Arrange the rocket on a large platter, top with seafood, tomatoes and orange segments. Whisk the dressing ingredients together and pour over the seafood.

Serves 4

Grilled lamb pittas with fresh mint salad

1 kg lean minced lamb
60 g (1 cup) finely chopped parsley
25 g (½ cup) finely chopped mint
1 onion, finely chopped
1 garlic clove, crushed
1 egg
1 teaspoon chilli sauce
4 small wholemeal pitta pockets

Mint salad
3 small vine-ripened tomatoes
1 small red onion, finely sliced
20 g (1 cup) mint
1 tablespoon olive oil
2 tablespoons lemon juice

plain yoghurt, optional

Place the lamb, parsley, mint, onion, garlic, egg and chilli sauce in a bowl and mix together. Shape into eight small patties. Chill for 30 minutes. Preheat the oven to 160°C (315°F/ Gas 2–3).

To make the mint salad, slice the tomatoes into thin rings and place in a bowl with the onion, mint, olive oil and lemon juice. Season well with salt and pepper. Gently toss to coat.

Wrap the pitta breads in foil and warm in the oven for 5–10 minutes.

Heat a chargrill or hot plate and brush with a little oil. When very hot, cook the patties for 3 minutes on each side. Do not turn until a nice crust has formed on the base or they will fall apart.

Remove the pitta breads from the oven. Cut the pockets in half, fill each half with some mint salad and a lamb patty. Serve with some plain yoghurt, if desired.

Serves 4

Blackened chicken with crispy tortillas

4 vine-ripened tomatoes, cut into
  1 cm slices
1 teaspoon caster sugar
1 red onion, sliced
150 ml olive oil
1 ripe avocado
60 g (¼ cup) sour cream
100 ml milk
2 tablespoons lime juice
2 x 16 cm corn tortillas
1 teaspoon dried oregano
2½ teaspoons ground cumin
1¼ teaspoons garlic salt
½ teaspoon cayenne pepper
4 small skinless chicken breast fillets
  (about 600 g)
15 g (½ cup) coriander leaves

Place the tomato slices in a wide dish, sprinkle with sugar and season well. Layer the onion over the top and drizzle with 60 ml (¼ cup) of oil. Chill for 20 minutes.

Blend the avocado, sour cream, milk, lime juice and 80 ml (⅓ cup) water in a food processor for 1 minute or until smooth. Season.

Cut each of the corn tortillas into eight 2 cm strips. Combine the oregano, cumin, garlic salt and cayenne pepper, and coat the chicken breasts in the spice mixture, pressing down firmly with your fingers. Heat 1½ tablespoons of oil over medium–high heat in a large, non-stick frying pan until hot. Cook the chicken breasts for 4–5 minutes on each side, or until cooked through. Cool, then refrigerate. In the same pan add 60 ml (¼ cup) of oil. Fry the tortilla strips until golden, turning once during cooking.

On each plate arrange the tomato and onion slices in a small circle. Slice each chicken breast on the diagonal into 2 cm pieces and arrange over the tomato. Spoon the dressing over the chicken and arrange four tortilla strips over the top. Sprinkle with coriander leaves and serve immediately.

Serves 4

Salmon fillets with lemon hollandaise sauce

Lemon hollandaise sauce
175 g butter
4 egg yolks
2 tablespoons lemon juice

2 tablespoons olive oil
4 salmon fillets with skin on

Melt the butter in a small saucepan over low heat. Skim any froth from the surface and discard. Leave to cool. Whisk the yolks and 2 tablespoons water in a separate small saucepan for 30 seconds, or until pale and foamy. Place the saucepan over very low heat and whisk the egg mixture for 2–3 minutes, or until it is frothy and the whisk leaves a trail behind it as you whisk. Don't let the saucepan get too hot or you will scramble the eggs. Remove from the heat.

Add the cooled butter to the eggs, a little at a time, whisking well after each addition. Avoid using the milky whey from the base of the saucepan. Stir in the lemon juice and season with salt and cracked black pepper.

Heat the oil in a large non-stick frying pan over high heat and cook the salmon fillets skin-side-down for 2 minutes. Turn over and cook for 2 minutes, or until cooked to your liking. Serve with the sauce and vegetables of your choice.

Serves 4

Spaghetti Niçoise

350 g spaghetti
8 quail eggs (or 4 hen eggs)
1 lemon
3 x 185 g tins good-quality tuna in oil
50 g (⅓ cup) stoned and halved
  Kalamata olives
100 g semi-dried (sun-blushed)
  tomatoes, halved lengthways
4 anchovy fillets, chopped into small
  pieces
3 tablespoons baby capers, drained
3 tablespoons chopped flat-leaf
  parsley

Cook the pasta in a large saucepan of boiling water until *al dente*. Meanwhile, place the eggs in a saucepan of cold water, bring to the boil and cook for 4 minutes (10 minutes for hen eggs). Drain, cool under cold water, then peel. Cut the quail eggs into halves or the hen eggs into quarters. Finely grate the zest of the lemon to give 1 teaspoon of grated zest. Then, squeeze the lemon to give 2 tablespoons juice.

Empty the tuna and its oil into a large bowl. Add the olives, tomato halves, anchovies, lemon zest and juice, capers and 2 tablespoons of the parsley. Drain the pasta and rinse in a little cold water, then toss gently through the tuna mixture. Divide among the serving bowls, garnish with egg and the remaining chopped parsley, and serve.

Serves 4–6

Smoked chicken and pasta salad with mustard dressing

1 tablespoon balsamic vinegar
150 ml olive oil
1 tablespoon lemon juice
3 tablespoons wholegrain mustard
200 g bucatini
450 g good-quality smoked chicken
  breast
8 small radishes
2 small Fuji apples
4 spring onions, finely sliced
35 g rocket

Combine the vinegar, olive oil, lemon juice and mustard in a screw-top jar, and shake well to combine. Season to taste with salt and pepper. Bring a large saucepan of salted water to the boil, and cook the bucatini according to the packet instructions until *al dente*. Drain, rinse under cold water and drain again. Toss one-third of the dressing through the bucatini and set aside for 30 minutes.

Cut the chicken breast on the diagonal and place in a large bowl. Thinly slice the radishes and add to the chicken. Quarter, core and cube the apples without peeling them, and add to the chicken with the sliced spring onion and rocket. Pour in the remaining dressing and toss lightly.

Gently mix the pasta with the smoked chicken until well combined. Divide the salad among four serving dishes and serve with fresh, crusty bread. May be served cold as a light meal or entrée.

Serves 4

Notes: Bucatini is a thick, spaghetti-like pasta with a hollow centre. It has a chewy texture.
Smoked chicken often has a dark skin. You may wish to remove this to improve the appearance of the salad.

Prosciutto and vegetable pasta bake

3 tablespoons olive oil
35 g (⅓ cup) dried breadcrumbs
250 g pasta shapes
6 thin slices prosciutto, chopped
1 red onion, chopped
1 red capsicum (pepper), chopped
100 g (½ cup) semi-dried (sun-
    blushed) tomatoes,
    roughly chopped
3 tablespoons shredded basil
100 g (1 cup) grated fresh Parmesan
    cheese
4 eggs, lightly beaten
250 ml (1 cup) milk

Preheat the oven to 180°C (350°F/ Gas 4). Grease a 25 cm round ovenproof dish with a little of the olive oil and sprinkle the dish with 2 tablespoons of the breadcrumbs to coat the base and side. Cook the pasta in a large saucepan of boiling water until *al dente*. Drain and transfer to a large bowl.

Heat 1 tablespoon of the remaining oil in a large frying pan. Add the prosciutto and onion and cook over medium heat for 4–5 minutes, or until softened and golden in colour. Add the capsicum and semi-dried tomato and cook for a further 1–2 minutes. Add to the pasta with the basil and Parmesan and toss together. Spoon the mixture into the prepared dish.

Place the eggs and milk in a bowl, whisk together, then season with salt and pepper. Pour the egg mixture over the pasta. Season the remaining breadcrumbs, add the remaining oil and toss together. Sprinkle the seasoned breadcrumb mixture over the pasta. Bake for 40 minutes, or until set. Allow to stand for 5 minutes, then cut into wedges and serve with a green salad, if desired.

Serves 6–8

Tuna and white bean salad

400 g tuna steaks
1 small red onion, thinly sliced
1 tomato, seeded and chopped
1 small red capsicum (pepper), thinly
  sliced
2 x 400 g tins cannellini beans
2 garlic cloves, crushed
1 teaspoon chopped thyme
4 tablespoons finely chopped flat-leaf
  parsley
1½ tablespoons lemon juice
80 ml (⅓ cup) extra virgin olive oil
1 teaspoon honey
olive oil, for brushing
100 g rocket
1 teaspoon lemon zest

Place the tuna steaks on a plate, sprinkle with cracked black pepper on both sides, cover with plastic and refrigerate until needed.

Combine the onion, tomato and capsicum in a large bowl. Rinse the cannellini beans under cold running water for 30 seconds, drain and add to the bowl with the garlic, thyme and 3 tablespoons of the parsley.

Place the lemon juice, oil and honey in a small saucepan, bring to the boil, then simmer, stirring, for 1 minute, or until the honey dissolves. Remove from the heat.

Brush a barbecue or chargrill with olive oil, and heat until very hot. Cook the tuna for 1 minute on each side. The meat should still be pink in the middle. Slice into 3 cm cubes and combine with the salad. Pour on the warm dressing and toss well.

Place the rocket on a platter. Top with the salad, season and garnish with the zest and remaining parsley.

Serves 4–6

Thai noodle salad

Dressing
2 tablespoons grated fresh ginger
2 tablespoons soy sauce
2 tablespoons sesame oil
80 ml (⅓ cup) red wine vinegar
1 tablespoon sweet chilli sauce
2 garlic cloves, crushed
80 ml (⅓ cup) kecap manis

500 g cooked large prawns
250 g dried instant egg noodles
5 spring onions, sliced diagonally
2 tablespoons chopped coriander
1 red capsicum (pepper), diced
100 g snow peas (mangetout), sliced

For the dressing, whisk together the fresh ginger, soy sauce, sesame oil, red wine vinegar, chilli sauce, garlic and kecap manis in a large bowl.

Peel the prawns and gently pull out the dark vein from each prawn back, starting at the head end. Cut each prawn in half lengthways.

Cook the egg noodles in a saucepan of boiling water for 2 minutes, or until tender, then drain thoroughly. Cool in a large bowl.

Add the dressing, prawns and remaining ingredients to the noodles and toss gently. Can be served with lime wedges.

Serves 4

Prawn and fennel salad

1.25 kg raw large prawns, peeled and
  deveined
1 large fennel bulb, thinly sliced
  (400 g)
300 g watercress
2 tablespoons finely chopped chives
125 ml (½ cup) extra virgin olive oil
60 ml (¼ cup) lemon juice
1 tablespoon Dijon mustard
1 large garlic clove, finely chopped

Bring a saucepan of water to the boil,
then add the prawns, return to the
boil and simmer for 2 minutes, or until
the prawns turn pink and are cooked
through. Drain and leave to cool. Pat
the prawns dry with paper towels and
slice in half lengthways. Place in a
large serving bowl.

Add the fennel, watercress and chives
to the bowl and mix well.

To make the dressing, whisk the
oil, lemon juice, mustard and garlic
together until combined. Pour the
dressing over the salad, season with
salt and cracked black pepper and
toss gently. Arrange the salad on
serving plates and serve immediately.

Serves 4

Somen noodle salad with sesame dressing

Sesame dressing
40 g (1/3 cup) sesame seeds, toasted
2 1/2 tablespoons shoyu or light
 soy sauce
2 tablespoons rice vinegar
2 teaspoons sugar
1/2 teaspoon grated fresh ginger
1/2 teaspoon dashi granules

125 g dried somen noodles
100 g snow peas (mangetout), finely
 sliced on the diagonal
100 g daikon radish, julienned
100 g (1 small) carrot, julienned
1 spring onion, sliced on the diagonal
50 g baby English spinach leaves,
 trimmed
2 teaspoons toasted sesame seeds

To make the dressing, place the sesame seeds in a mortar and pestle and grind until fine and moist. Combine the soy sauce, rice vinegar, sugar, ginger, dashi granules and 125 ml (1/2 cup) water in a small saucepan and bring to the boil over high heat. Reduce the heat to medium and simmer, stirring, for 2 minutes, or until the dashi granules have dissolved. Remove from the heat. Cool. Gradually combine with the ground sesame seeds, stirring to form a thick dressing.

Cook the noodles in a large saucepan of boiling water for 2 minutes, or until tender. Drain, rinse under cold water and cool completely. Cut into 10 cm lengths using scissors.

Place the snow peas in a large shallow bowl with the daikon, carrot, spring onion, English spinach leaves and the noodles. Add the dressing and toss well to combine. Place in the refrigerator until ready to serve. Just before serving, sprinkle the top with the toasted sesame seeds.

Serves 4

Barbecued tuna and Mediterranean vegetables

185 ml (¾ cup) olive oil
3 garlic cloves, crushed
2 tablespoons sweet chilli sauce
1 red capsicum (pepper), cut into
   3 cm pieces
1 yellow capsicum (pepper), cut into
   3 cm pieces
2 large zucchini (courgettes), cut into
   1.5 cm slices
2 long, thin eggplants (aubergines),
   cut into 1.5 cm slices
olive oil, extra, for brushing
4 tuna steaks

Lemon and caper mayonnaise
1 egg yolk
1 teaspoon grated lemon zest
2 tablespoons lemon juice
1 small garlic clove, chopped
185 ml (¾ cup) olive oil
1 tablespoon baby capers, rinsed
   and drained

Combine the olive oil, garlic and sweet chilli sauce. Add the capsicum, zucchini and eggplant, toss well, then marinate for 30 minutes.

For the mayonnaise, process the egg yolk, zest, lemon juice and garlic in a food processor or blender until smooth. With the motor running, gradually add the oil in a thin steady stream until the mixture thickens and is a creamy consistency. Stir in the capers and ½ teaspoon salt.

Heat the barbecue or a chargrill plate, brush with oil and cook the drained vegetables for 4–5 minutes each side, or until cooked through. Keep warm.

Brush the tuna steaks with extra oil and barbecue for 2–3 minutes each side, or until just cooked (tuna should be rare in the centre). Arrange the vegetables and tuna steaks on serving plates and serve with the lemon and caper mayonnaise.

Serves 4

Stracci with artichokes and chargrilled chicken

1 tablespoon olive oil
3 chicken breast fillets
500 g stracci pasta
8 slices prosciutto
280 g jar artichokes in oil, drained and quartered, oil reserved
150 g semi-dried (sunblushed) tomatoes, thinly sliced
80 g baby rocket
2–3 tablespoons balsamic vinegar

Lightly brush a chargrill or frying pan with the oil and heat over high heat. Cook the chicken for 6–8 minutes each side, or until cooked through. Cut into thin slices on the diagonal.

Cook the pasta in a large saucepan of boiling water until *al dente*.

Meanwhile, place the prosciutto on a lined grill tray and cook under a hot grill for 2 minutes each side, or until crisp. Cool slightly and break into pieces. Drain the pasta, then combine with the chicken, prosciutto, artichokes, tomato and rocket in a bowl and toss. Whisk together 60 ml (¼ cup) of the reserved artichoke oil and the balsamic vinegar and toss through the pasta mixture. Season to taste with salt and cracked black pepper, then serve.

Serves 6

Goat's cheese tart

Pastry
125 g (1 cup) plain flour
60 ml (¼ cup) olive oil

Filling
1 tablespoon olive oil
2 onions, thinly sliced
1 teaspoon thyme leaves
125 g ricotta cheese
100 g goat's cheese
2 tablespoons pitted Niçoise olives
1 egg, lightly beaten
60 ml (¼ cup) cream

For the pastry, sift the flour and a pinch of salt into a large bowl and make a well. Add the olive oil and mix with a flat-bladed knife until crumbly. Gradually add 3–4 tablespoons cold water until the mixture comes together. Remove and pat together to form a disc. Chill for 30 minutes.

For the filling, heat the olive oil in a frying pan. Add the onion, cover and cook over low heat for 30 minutes. Season and stir in half the thyme. Cool slightly.

Preheat the oven to 180° C (350°F/ Gas 4). Lightly flour the work bench and roll out the pastry to a 30 cm circle. Evenly spread the onion over the pastry, leaving a 2 cm border. Sprinkle the ricotta and the goat's cheese evenly over the onion. Place the olives over the cheeses, then sprinkle with the remaining thyme. Fold the pastry border in to the edge of the filling, gently pleating as you go.

Combine the egg and cream, then carefully pour over the filling. Bake on a heated baking tray on the lower half of the oven for 45 minutes, or until the pastry is golden. Serve warm or at room temperature.

Serves 6

Chermoula prawns

Chermoula
80 ml (⅓ cup) virgin olive oil
3 tablespoons chopped coriander
  leaves
2 tablespoons chopped flat-leaf
  parsley
2 tablespoons chopped preserved
  lemon rind
2 tablespoons lemon juice
2 garlic cloves, chopped
1 small red chilli, seeded and finely
  chopped
1 teaspoon ground cumin
½ teaspoon paprika

20 raw medium prawns
370 g (2 cups) instant couscous
375 ml (1½ cups) boiling chicken
  stock
1 tablespoon olive oil
2 tablespoons shredded mint leaves

Process the chermoula ingredients to
a coarse purée, then season with salt.

Peel and devein the prawns, keeping
the tails intact. Thread a cocktail stick
through the body of each prawn to
keep them straight, then place them
in a dish and spoon the chermoula
over them, turning to coat. Chill the
prawns, covered, for 30 minutes,
turning occasionally.

Place the couscous in a heatproof
bowl, pour on the boiling stock and
oil, cover and leave for 3–4 minutes.
Fluff the couscous with a fork and stir
in the mint.

Arrange the prawns on a foil-lined
grill tray and cook under a hot grill
for 2–3 minutes each side, or until
pink and cooked. Divide the couscous
and prawns among four plates.

Serves 4

Pan bagnat

4 crusty bread rolls, or 1 baguette
   sliced into 4 chunks
1 garlic clove
60 ml (¼ cup) olive oil
1 tablespoon red wine vinegar
3 tablespoons basil leaves, torn
2 tomatoes, sliced
2 hard-boiled eggs, sliced
75 g tin tuna
8 anchovy fillets
1 small cucumber, sliced
½ green capsicum (pepper), thinly
   sliced
1 French shallot, thinly sliced

Slice the bread rolls in half and
remove some of the soft centre from
the tops. Cut the garlic clove in half
and rub the insides of the rolls with
the cut sides. Sprinkle both sides of
the bread with olive oil, vinegar, salt
and pepper.

Place all the salad ingredients on the
base of the rolls, cover with the other
half and wrap each sandwich in foil.
Press firmly with a light weight, such
as a tin of food, and leave in a cool
place for 1 hour before serving.

Serves 4

Salmon with miso and soy noodles

300 g soba noodles
1 tablespoon soy bean oil
3 teaspoons white miso paste
100 ml honey
1½ tablespoons sesame oil
6 salmon fillets, boned and skin
  removed
1 teaspoon chopped garlic
1 tablespoon grated fresh ginger
1 carrot, julienned
6 small spring onions, thinly sliced
70 g (1 cup) soya bean sprouts
80 ml (⅓ cup) rice vinegar
3 tablespoons light soy sauce
1 teaspoon sesame oil, extra
1 tablespoon toasted sesame seeds

mustard cress

Preheat the oven to 180°C (350°F/ Gas 4). Fill a large saucepan three-quarters full with water and bring to the boil. Add the soba noodles and return to the boil. Cook for 1 minute, then add 250 ml (1 cup) cold water. Boil for 1–2 minutes, then add another 250 ml (1 cup) water. Boil for 2 minutes, or until tender, then drain and toss with ½ teaspoon of the soy bean oil.

Combine the miso, honey, sesame oil and 1 tablespoon water to form a paste. Brush over the salmon, then sear on a hot chargrill for 30 seconds on each side. Brush the salmon with the remaining paste and place on a baking tray. Bake for 6 minutes, then cover and rest in a warm place.

Heat the remaining soy oil in a wok. Add the garlic, ginger, carrot, spring onion and sprouts, and stir-fry for 1 minute — the vegetables should not brown, but remain crisp and bright. Add the noodles, rice vinegar, soy sauce and extra sesame oil and stir-fry quickly to heat through.

Divide the noodles among six serving plates and top with a portion of salmon and sprinkle with the sesame seeds. Garnish with the mustard cress and serve.

Serves 6

Sides

Greek salad

4 tomatoes, cut into wedges
1 telegraph cucumber, peeled,
   halved, seeded and cut into small
   cubes
2 green capsicums (peppers),
   seeded, halved lengthways and
   cut into strips
1 red onion, finely sliced
16 Kalamata olives
250 g firm feta cheese, cut into cubes
3 tablespoons flat-leaf parsley
12 whole mint leaves
125 ml (½ cup) olive oil
2 tablespoons lemon juice
1 garlic clove, crushed

Place the tomato wedges, cucumber, capsicum strips, onion, Kalamata olives, feta and half of the parsley and mint leaves in a large serving bowl, and toss together gently.

Place the oil, lemon juice and garlic in a screw-top jar, season, and shake until well combined. Pour the dressing over the salad and toss. Garnish with the remaining parsley and mint.

Serves 4

Tuscan bread salad

200 g ciabatta bread
8 vine-ripened tomatoes
80 ml (⅓ cup) olive oil
1 tablespoon lemon juice
1½ tablespoons red wine vinegar
6 anchovy fillets, finely chopped
1 tablespoon baby capers, rinsed,
    drained and finely chopped
1 garlic clove, crushed
30 g (1 cup) basil leaves

Preheat the oven to 220°C (425°F/ Gas 7). Tear the bread into 2 cm pieces, spread on a baking tray and bake for 5–7 minutes, or until golden on the outside. Leave the toasted bread on a cake rack to cool.

Score a cross in the base of each tomato. Place in a heatproof bowl and cover with boiling water. Leave for 30 seconds then transfer to cold water and peel the skin away from the cross. Cut four of the tomatoes in half and squeeze the juice and seeds into a bowl, reserving and chopping the flesh. Add the oil, juice, vinegar, anchovies, capers and garlic to the tomato juice, and season.

Seed and slice the remaining tomatoes, and place in a large bowl with the reserved tomato and most of the basil. Add the dressing and toasted bread, and toss. Garnish with the remaining basil, season, and leave for at least 15 minutes. Serve at room temperature.

Serves 6

Chargrilled vegetable salad with balsamic dressing

4 baby eggplants (aubergines)
5 Roma (plum) tomatoes
2 red capsicums (peppers)
1 green capsicum (pepper)
2 zucchini (courgettes)
100 ml olive oil
12 bocconcini or small, fresh
  mozarella
45 g (1/2 cup) Ligurian olives
1 garlic clove, finely chopped
3 teaspoons baby capers, rinsed
  and drained
1/2 teaspoon sugar
2 tablespoons balsamic vinegar

Cut the eggplant and tomatoes in half lengthways. Cut the red and green capsicums in half lengthways, remove the seeds and membrane then cut each half into three pieces. Thinly slice the zucchini on the diagonal.

Preheat a chargrill pan to hot. Add 1 tablespoon of oil and cook a quarter of the vegetables (cook the tomatoes cut-side down first) for 2–3 minutes, or until marked and golden. Place in a large bowl.

Cook the remaining vegetables in batches until tender, adding more oil as needed. Transfer to the bowl and add the baby bocconcini. Mix the olives, garlic, capers, sugar, vinegar and remaining oil (about 2 tablespoons). Pour over the salad and toss. Season with pepper.

Serves 4–6

Green salad with lemon vinaigrette

150 g baby cos lettuce
150 g small butter lettuce
50 g watercress
100 g rocket
1 tablespoon finely chopped French
  shallots
2 teaspoons Dijon mustard
½ teaspoon sugar
1 tablespoon finely chopped basil
1 teaspoon grated lemon zest
3 teaspoons lemon juice
1 tablespoon white wine vinegar
25 ml lemon oil
75 ml virgin olive oil

Remove the outer leaves from the cos and butter lettuces and separate the core leaves. Wash in cold water, place in a colander to drain, then refrigerate. Pinch or trim the stalks from the watercress and rocket, pat dry in a tea towel and chill with the lettuce.

To make the dressing, whisk together the shallots, mustard, sugar, basil, lemon zest, lemon juice and vinegar in a bowl until well blended. Place the oils in a small jug and slowly add to the bowl in a thin stream, whisking constantly to create a smooth, creamy dressing. Season to taste with salt and pepper.

Place the salad greens in a large bowl. Drizzle the dressing over the salad and toss gently to coat.

Serves 6

Mushroom and goat's cheese salad

Dressing
2 tablespoons lemon juice
3 tablespoons olive oil
1 teaspoon grated lemon zest

8 large cap mushrooms, stems
   removed
1 tablespoon chopped thyme
4 garlic cloves, finely chopped
2 tablespoons olive oil
50 g (4 cups) baby rocket
100 g goat's cheese
2 tablespoons chopped flat-leaf
   parsley

Preheat the oven to 200°C (400°F/
Gas 6). For the dressing, combine
the juice, oil and zest in a small bowl.

Place the mushrooms on a large
baking tray, sprinkle with thyme and
garlic, then drizzle with olive oil. Cover
with foil and roast for 20 minutes.
Remove the mushrooms from the
oven and toss to combine the
flavours. Re-cover and roast for a
further 10 minutes or until cooked.
Remove the mushrooms from the
oven and cut in half.

Place the rocket on a serving platter,
top with the mushrooms and crumble
the goat's cheese over the top.
Whisk the dressing to ensure it is
well combined and drizzle over the
salad. Serve sprinkled with parsley.

Serves 4–6

Roasted tomato and bocconcini salad

8 Roma (plum) tomatoes, halved
pinch of sugar
125 ml (½ cup) olive oil
15 g (¼ cup) torn basil
2 tablespoons balsamic vinegar
350 g cherry bocconcini or baby
   fresh mozarella
160 g mizuna lettuce

sea salt

Preheat the oven to 150°C (300°F/ Gas 2). Place the tomato, cut-side-up, on a rack over a baking tray lined with baking paper. Sprinkle with salt, cracked black pepper, and a pinch of sugar. Roast for 2 hours, then remove from the oven and allow to cool.

Combine the oil and basil in a saucepan, and stir gently over medium heat for 3–5 minutes, or until it is very hot, but not smoking. Remove from the heat and discard the basil. Mix 2 tablespoons of oil with the vinegar.

Toss together the tomato, bocconcini and lettuce. Arrange the salad in a shallow serving bowl and drizzle with the dressing. Sprinkle with sea salt and cracked black pepper.

Serves 6

Notes: If cherry bocconcini are unavailable, use regular bocconcini cut into quarters.
Leftover basil oil can be stored in a clean jar in the refrigerator, and is great in pasta sauces.

Caramelised onion and potato salad

oil, for cooking
6 red onions, thinly sliced
1 kg Kipfler or new potatoes,
  unpeeled
4 rashers streaky bacon, rind
  removed
30 g (2/3 cup) chives, snipped

Mayonnaise
250 g (1 cup) whole-egg mayonnaise
1 tablespoon Dijon mustard
juice of 1 lemon
2 tablespoons sour cream

Heat 2 tablespoons of oil in a large heavy-based frying pan, add the onion and cook over medium–low heat for 40 minutes, or until soft and caramelised.

Cut the potatoes into large chunks (if they are small leave them whole). Cook in boiling water for 10 minutes, or until just tender, then drain and cool slightly. (Do not overcook the potatoes or they will fall apart.)

Grill the bacon until crisp, drain on paper towels and cool slightly before coarsely chopping.

Put the potato, onion and chives in a large bowl, reserving a few chives for a garnish, and mix well.

To make the mayonnaise, put the whole-egg mayonnaise, mustard, lemon juice and sour cream in a bowl and whisk to combine. Pour over the salad and toss to coat. Sprinkle with the bacon and garnish with the reserved chives.

Serves 10

Spinach salad with bacon and quail eggs

12 quail eggs
2 teaspoons oil
4 rashers good-quality back bacon,
  cut into thin strips
300 g baby English spinach leaves
200 g cherry tomatoes, halved
100 g (²/₃ cup) pine nuts, toasted

Dressing
60 ml (¼ cup) apple cider vinegar
3 garlic cloves, crushed
2 teaspoons Dijon mustard
2 teaspoons maple syrup
1 teaspoon Worcestershire sauce
60 ml (¼ cup) olive oil

Bring a small saucepan of water to the boil, gently add the quail eggs and simmer for 1½ minutes. Drain, then refresh under cold running water until cool, and peel the eggs.

Heat the oil in a non-stick frying pan over medium heat, add the bacon and cook for 5–6 minutes, or until crisp. Drain on paper towels, retaining the drippings in the pan.

Wash the spinach in cold water and remove the stems. Wrap the leaves loosely in a clean tea towel to remove any excess water. Place in a salad bowl, tearing the larger leaves if necessary, then add the tomatoes, bacon and pine nuts. Halve the eggs and scatter over the salad.

Reheat the bacon fat over medium heat, then add the vinegar, garlic, mustard, maple syrup and Worcestershire sauce. Shake the pan over the heat, for 2 minutes, or until bubbling, then add the oil and heat for another minute. Pour the warm dressing over the salad, season to taste and serve.

Serves 4–6

Tabbouleh

175 g (1 cup) burghul (bulgar)
200 g flat-leaf parsley, or 100 g
   parsley and 100 g rocket
80 g mint
6 spring onions, finely sliced
2 tomatoes, finely chopped
2 large garlic cloves, finely chopped
80 ml (1/3 cup) lemon juice
125 ml (1/2 cup) extra virgin olive oil

Place the burghul in a large bowl and add enough hot water to cover. Leave to soak for 15–20 minutes or until tender. Drain well.

Finely chop the parsley and mint, and combine in a large bowl with the drained burghul, spring onion and chopped tomato.

Mix the garlic and lemon juice together in a small jug. Whisk in the oil until it is well combined, and season to taste with salt and black pepper. Toss the dressing through the salad before serving.

Serves 6–8

Variation: Add 40 g (1/4 cup) toasted pine nuts with the burghul.

Fresh beetroot and goat's cheese salad

1 kg (4 bulbs with leaves) fresh
  beetroot
200 g green beans
1 tablespoon red wine vinegar
2 tablespoons extra virgin olive oil
1 garlic clove, crushed
1 tablespoon capers in brine, rinsed,
  drained and coarsely chopped
100 g goat's cheese

Trim the leaves from the beetroot. Scrub the bulbs and wash the leaves well. Bring a large saucepan of water to the boil, add the beetroot, then reduce the heat and simmer, covered, for 30 minutes, or until tender when pierced with the point of a knife. (The cooking time may vary depending on the size of the bulbs.) Drain and cool. Peel the skins off the beetroot and cut the bulbs into wedges.

Meanwhile, bring a saucepan of water to the boil, add the beans and cook for 3 minutes, or until just tender. Remove with tongs and plunge into a bowl of cold water. Drain well. Add the beetroot leaves to the boiling water and cook for 3–5 minutes, or until the leaves and stems are tender. Drain, plunge into a bowl of cold water, then drain again well.

To make the dressing, put the vinegar, oil, garlic, capers, 1/2 teaspoon salt and 1/2 teaspoon cracked black pepper in a jar and shake well. Divide the beans and beetroot wedges and leaves among four plates. Crumble the goat's cheese over the top and drizzle with the dressing.

Serves 4

Watercress, feta and watermelon salad

2 tablespoons sunflower seeds
475 g rindless watermelon, cut into
  1 cm cubes
180 g feta cheese, cut into 1 cm
  cubes
75 g (2½ cups) watercress sprigs
2 tablespoons olive oil
1 tablespoon lemon juice
2 teaspoons chopped oregano

Heat a small frying pan over high heat. Add the sunflower seeds and, shaking the pan continuously, dry-fry for 2 minutes, or until they are toasted and lightly golden.

Place the watermelon, feta and watercress leaves in a large serving dish and toss gently to combine. Combine the olive oil, lemon juice and chopped oregano in a small jug, and season to taste with a little salt and freshly ground black pepper (don't add too much salt as the feta is already quite salty). Pour the dressing over the salad and toss together well. Scatter with the toasted sunflower seeds, and serve.

Serves 4

Pear and walnut salad with blue cheese dressing

Dressing
100 g creamy blue cheese
60 ml (¼ cup) olive oil
1 tablespoon walnut oil
1 tablespoon lemon juice
1 tablespoon cream
2 teaspoons finely chopped sage

100 g (1 cup) walnut halves
4 firm, ripe small pears, such as
    Corella
2 tablespoons lemon juice
2 witlof (chicory), trimmed and leaves
    separated
100 g Parmesan cheese, shaved

To make the dressing, purée the blue cheese in a small processor, then add the olive oil, walnut oil and lemon juice, and blend until smooth. With the motor running, slowly add 2 teaspoons warm water. Stir in the cream and sage, and season to taste.

Preheat the grill to medium–hot. Place the walnuts in a bowl and cover with boiling water. Allow to steep for 1 minute, then drain. Spread the walnuts on a baking tray and place under the grill for 3 minutes, or until lightly toasted. Chop coarsely.

Thinly slice across the pears through the core to make rounds. Do not peel or core the pears, but discard the seeds. As each pear is sliced, sprinkle with a little lemon juice to prevent discoloration. On each serving plate, arrange three pear slices in a circle. Top with a scattering of walnuts, a couple of endive leaves, a few more walnuts and some Parmesan. Repeat this layering, reserving the last layer of Parmesan and some of the walnuts. Spoon some dressing over each stack, scatter with the remaining walnuts, and top each with the reserved Parmesan. Serve as a first course, or as an accompaniment to simple meat dishes.

Serves 4

Broad bean, mint and bacon salad

600 g frozen broad beans (see Notes)
150 g shredded butter or cos lettuce
35 g (³/₄ cup) shredded mint
250 g Kasseler or pancetta
1 tablespoon olive oil
1½ teaspoons Dijon mustard
1 teaspoon sugar
2 tablespoons white wine vinegar
60 ml (¼ cup) extra virgin olive oil
4 flatbreads to serve (eg pitta breads)

Blanch the beans, according to packet instructions. Drain, rinse under cold water, and peel. Place in a large bowl with the lettuce and mint.

Slice the Kasseler into thick slices, then into 2 cm chunks. Heat the oil in a heavy-based frying pan and cook the Kasseler for 3–4 minutes, or until golden. Add to the bean mixture.

Combine the mustard, sugar and vinegar in a jug. Whisk in the extra virgin oil until well combined and season with salt and freshly ground black pepper. Pile the salad onto fresh or lightly toasted flatbread to serve.

Serves 4

Notes: If they are in season, you may like to use fresh broad beans. You will need about 1.8 kg of beans in the pod to give 600 g of beans. Boil the beans for 2 minutes and peel before using them.
Kasseler is a traditional German speciality. It is a cured and smoked loin of pork that comes in a single piece and should be available at good delicatessens.

Radicchio with figs and ginger vinaigrette

1 radicchio
1 small curly endive lettuce (see Note)
3 oranges
1/2 small red onion, thinly sliced into rings
8 small green figs, quartered
3 tablespoons extra virgin olive oil
1 teaspoon red wine vinegar
1/8 teaspoon ground cinnamon
2 tablespoons orange juice
2 tablespoons very finely chopped glacé ginger with syrup
2 pomegranates, optional

Wash the radicchio and curly endive leaves in cold water, and drain well. Tear any large leaves into pieces.

Peel and segment the oranges, discarding all of the pith. Place in a large bowl with the onion rings, salad leaves and figs, reserving 8 fig quarters.

Combine the olive oil, vinegar, cinnamon, orange juice and ginger in a small jug. Season to taste with salt and pepper. Pour over the salad and toss lightly.

Arrange the reserved figs in pairs over the salad. If you are using the pomegranates, slice them in half and scoop out the seeds with a spoon. Scatter these over the salad before serving.

Serves 4

Note: Curly endive is also known as frisée lettuce.
Variation: A delicious alternative for this salad is to replace the oranges and orange juice with mandarins and mandarin juice when in season.

Egg salad with creamy dressing

10 large eggs, at room temperature
1 egg yolk
3 teaspoons lemon juice
2 teaspoons Dijon mustard
70 ml olive oil
70 ml oil
2 tablespoons chopped dill
30 ml crème fraîche or sour cream
2 tablespoons baby capers, rinsed
   and drained
20 g (⅓ cup) mustard cress

Place the eggs in a large saucepan of cold water. Bring to the boil and simmer gently for 10 minutes. Drain, then cool the eggs under cold running water. Remove the shells.

Place the egg yolk, lemon juice and Dijon mustard in a food processor or blender and season with salt and freshly ground black pepper. With the motor running, slowly add the combined olive oil and safflower oil, drop by drop at first, then slowly increasing the amount to a thin, steady stream as the mixture thickens. When all of the oil has been added, place the mayonnaise in a large bowl, and gently stir in the dill, crème fraîche and capers.

Roughly chop the eggs and fold into the mayonnaise. Transfer the salad to a serving bowl and use scissors to cut the green tips from the mustard cress. Scatter them over the salad and serve.

Serves 4

Serving suggestion: Serve the salad on slices of toasted bruschetta, draped with smoked salmon and topped with the mustard cress and extra black pepper.

Moroccan eggplant with couscous

185 g (1 cup) instant couscous
200 ml olive oil
1 onion, halved and sliced
1 eggplant (aubergine)
3 teaspoons ground cumin
1½ teaspoons garlic salt
¼ teaspoon ground cinnamon
1 teaspoon paprika
¼ teaspoon ground cloves
50 g butter
30 g (½ cup) roughly chopped parsley

Place the couscous in a large bowl and add 375 ml (1½ cups) boiling water. Leave for 10 minutes, then fluff up with a fork.

Add 2 tablespoons of oil to a large frying pan and cook the onion for 8–10 minutes, or until browned. Remove from the pan, retaining the remaining oil.

Cut the eggplant into 1 cm slices, then into quarters and place in a large bowl. Combine the cumin, garlic salt, cinnamon, paprika, cloves and ½ teaspoon salt, and sprinkle over the eggplant, tossing until it is well coated. Add the remaining oil to the pan and reheat over medium heat. Cook the eggplant, turning once, for 20–25 minutes, or until browned. Remove from the pan and cool.

Using the same pan, melt the butter, then add the couscous and cook for 2–3 minutes. Stir in the onion, eggplant and parsley, allow to cool, then serve.

Serves 4

Lentil salad

½ brown onion
2 cloves
300 g (1²/₃ cups) puy lentils (see Note)
1 strip lemon zest
2 garlic cloves, peeled
1 fresh bay leaf
2 teaspoons ground cumin
2 tablespoons red wine vinegar
60 ml (¼ cup) olive oil
1 tablespoon lemon juice
2 tablespoon mint leaves, finely
    chopped
3 spring onions, finely chopped

Stud the onion with the cloves and place in a saucepan with the lentils, zest, garlic, bay leaf, 1 teaspoon cumin and 875 ml (3½ cups) water. Bring to the boil and cook over medium heat for 25–30 minutes, or until the water has been absorbed. Discard the onion, zest and bay leaf. Reserve the garlic and finely chop.

Whisk together the vinegar, oil, juice, garlic and remaining cumin. Stir through the lentils with the mint and spring onion. Season well. Leave for 30 minutes to let the flavours absorb. Serve at room temperature.

Serves 4–6

Note: Puy lentils are small, green lentils from France. They are available dried from gourmet food stores.

Coleslaw

½ green cabbage
¼ red cabbage
3 carrots, coarsely grated
6 radishes, coarsely grated
1 red capsicum (pepper), chopped
4 spring onions, sliced
15 g (¼ cup) chopped parsley
250 g (1 cup) whole egg mayonnaise

Remove the hard core from the cabbages and shred the leaves with a sharp knife. Place in a large bowl and add the grated carrot, grated radish, red capsicum, spring onion and parsley to the bowl.

Add the mayonnaise, season to taste with salt and freshly ground black pepper and toss until well combined.

Serves 8–10

Note: Cover and refrigerate the chopped vegetables for up to 3 hours before serving. Add the mayonnaise just before serving.

Soba noodle salad with tahini dressing

200 g snake beans or green beans
200 g dry soba noodles
1 tablespoon tahini
1 small garlic clove, crushed
1½ tablespoons rice vinegar
1½ tablespoons olive oil
½ teaspoon sesame oil
1 teaspoon soy sauce
2 teaspoons sugar
2 spring onions, finely sliced
3 teaspoons black sesame seeds

Trim the beans, and cut into long strips on the diagonal. Place in a saucepan of boiling water and return to the boil for 2 minutes, or until tender. Drain and refresh under cold running water. Drain.

Cook the noodles in boiling water for 3–4 minutes, or until they are tender. Drain and refresh under cold water, then drain again.

Combine the tahini, crushed garlic, rice vinegar, olive oil, sesame oil, soy sauce, sugar and 2 teaspoons warm water in a screw-top jar. Shake well and season to taste.

Combine the beans, noodles, spring onion and sesame seeds in a serving bowl, add the dressing and toss lightly to combine. Serve immediately.

Serves 4–6

Note: Add the dressing as close to serving as possible, as it will be absorbed by the noodles.

Insalata Caprese

3 large vine-ripened tomatoes
250 g bocconcini (see Note)
12 basil leaves
60 ml (¼ cup) extra virgin olive oil
4 basil leaves, roughly torn, extra,
  optional

Slice the tomatoes into 1 cm slices, to make twelve slices altogether. Slice the bocconcini into twenty-four 1 cm slices.

Arrange the tomato slices on a serving plate, alternating them with two slices of bocconcini. Place the basil leaves between the bocconcini slices.

Drizzle with the oil, sprinkle with the basil, if desired, and season well with salt and ground black pepper.

Serves 4

Note: This popular salad is most successful with very fresh buffalo mozzarella if you can find it. We've used bocconcini in this recipe. These are small balls of fresh cow's milk mozarella.

Moroccan spiced carrot salad

4 large carrots
2 cardamom pods
1 teaspoon black mustard seeds
½ teaspoon ground cumin
½ teaspoon ground ginger
1 teaspoon paprika
½ teaspoon ground coriander
80 ml (⅓ cup) olive oil
1 tablespoon lemon juice
2 tablespoons orange juice
35 g (¼ cup) currants
25 g (½ cup) finely chopped coriander
2 tablespoons finely chopped
   pistachio nuts
1 teaspoon orange flower water
250 g (1 cup) thick plain yoghurt

Peel and coarsely grate the carrots, and place in a large bowl.

Crush the cardamom pods to extract the seeds. Discard the pods. Heat a frying pan over low heat, and cook the mustard seeds for a few seconds, or until they start to pop. Add the cumin, ginger, paprika, cardamom and ground coriander, and heat for 5 seconds, or until fragrant. Remove from the heat and stir in the oil, juices and currants until combined.

Pour the dressing over the carrot and leave for 30 minutes. Add the fresh coriander and toss to combine. Pile the salad onto a serving dish and garnish with the chopped pistachios. Mix the orange flower water and yoghurt, and serve separately.

Serves 4–6

Mixed salad with warm Brie dressing

½ sourdough baguette
165 ml extra virgin olive oil
6 rashers streaky bacon
2 garlic cloves, peeled
2 baby cos lettuce
90 g (2 cups) baby English
  spinach leaves
80 g (½ cup) pine nuts, toasted
2 French shallots, finely chopped
1 tablespoon Dijon mustard
80 ml (⅓ cup) sherry vinegar
300 g ripe Brie cheese, rind removed

Preheat the oven to 180°C (350°F/ Gas 4). Thinly slice the baguette on the diagonal. Use 2 tablespoons of oil to brush both sides of each slice, place on a baking tray and bake for 20 minutes, or until golden.

Place the bacon on a separate tray and bake for 3–5 minutes, or until crisp. Remove the bread from the oven and use one clove of garlic to rub the bread slices. Break the bacon into pieces and leave to cool.

Remove the outer leaves of the cos lettuce. Rinse the inner leaves well, drain, dry and place in a large bowl with the spinach. Add the bacon, croutons and pine nuts.

Place the remaining olive oil in a frying pan and heat gently. Add the shallots and cook until they soften, then crush the remaining clove of garlic and add to the pan. Whisk in the mustard and vinegar, then gently whisk in the chopped Brie, until it has melted. Remove the dressing from the heat and, while it is still warm, pour over the salad and toss gently.

Serves 4

Vegetable skewers with salsa verde

Salsa verde
1 garlic clove
1 tablespoon capers, rinsed
  and drained
20 g (1 cup) flat-leaf parsley
15 g (½ cup) basil leaves
10 g (½ cup) mint leaves
80 ml (⅓ cup) olive oil
1 teaspoon Dijon mustard
1 tablespoon red wine vinegar

16 small yellow squash (pattypan
  squash)
16 baby carrots, peeled
16 French shallots, peeled
1 large red capsicum (pepper), halved
  and cut into 2 cm thick slices
16 baby zucchini (courgettes)
2 garlic cloves, crushed
1 teaspoon chopped thyme
1 tablespoon olive oil
16 fresh bay or sage leaves

Soak 16 wooden skewers in cold water for 30 minutes to prevent them from burning during cooking.

To make the salsa verde, combine the garlic, capers and herbs in a food processor until the herbs are roughly chopped. With the motor running, pour the olive oil in a slow stream until incorporated. Combine the mustard with the red wine vinegar and stir through the salsa verde. Season. Cover with plastic wrap and refrigerate.

Blanch the vegetables separately in a large pot of boiling, salted water until just tender. Drain in a colander, then toss with the garlic, thyme and oil. Season well.

Thread the vegetables onto the skewers starting with a squash, then a French shallot, a bay leaf then the zucchini, carrot and capsicum. Repeat to make 16 skewers in total.

Place the skewers on a hot grill and cook for 3 minutes on each side, or until cooked and browned. Arrange on couscous or rice and serve with the salsa verde.

Serves 8

Roast tomato salad

6 Roma (plum) tomatoes
2 teaspoons capers, rinsed
   and drained
6 basil leaves, torn
1 tablespoon olive oil
1 tablespoon balsamic vinegar
2 garlic cloves, crushed
½ teaspoon honey

Cut the tomatoes lengthways into quarters. Place on a grill tray, skin-side-down, and cook under a hot grill for 4–5 minutes, or until golden. Cool to room temperature and place in a bowl.

Combine the capers, basil leaves, olive oil, balsamic vinegar, garlic cloves and honey in a bowl, season with salt and freshly ground black pepper, and pour over the tomatoes. Toss gently.

Serves 6

Bean salad

250 g green beans, trimmed
250 g yellow beans, trimmed
60 ml (¼ cup) olive oil
1 tablespoon lemon juice
1 garlic clove, crushed
shaved Parmesan cheese

Bring a saucepan of lightly salted
water to the boil. Add the green
and yellow beans, and cook for
2 minutes, or until just tender.
Plunge into cold water and drain.

Place the olive oil, lemon juice and
garlic in a bowl, season with salt and
freshly ground black pepper, and mix
together well. Place the beans in a
serving bowl, pour on the dressing
and toss to coat. Top with the
Parmesan and serve.

Serves 6

Dill potato salad

600 g desiree potatoes
2 eggs
2 tablespoons finely chopped dill
1½ tablespoons finely chopped
  French shallots
1 egg yolk
2 teaspoons lemon juice
1 teaspoon Dijon mustard
100 ml light olive oil

Bring a large saucepan of water to the boil. Cook the potatoes for 20 minutes, or until tender. Add the eggs for the last 10 minutes. Remove the potatoes and eggs, and allow to cool. Peel the potatoes, then cut into 2–3 cm cubes. Peel and chop the eggs. Place in a large bowl with the dill, eggs and shallots. Toss to combine, then season.

Place the egg yolk, lemon juice, mustard and a pinch of salt in the bowl of a food processor. With the motor running, gradually add the olive oil a few drops at a time. When about half the oil has been added, pour in the remaining oil in a steady stream until it has all been incorporated. Use a large metal spoon to gently combine the potato and mayonnaise, then serve.

Serves 4

Beetroot and sweet potato salad with feta

350 g fresh baby beetroot, trimmed
and washed
350 g orange sweet potato, peeled
and cut into 2 cm chunks
60 ml (¼ cup) garlic oil (see Note)
1 garlic bulb
3 tablespoons olive oil
20 g butter
1 red onion, cut into 1 cm wedges
1 tablespoon balsamic vinegar
1 teaspoon soft brown sugar
2 tablespoons lemon juice
1 tablespoon shredded basil
150 g baby English spinach leaves
2 sprigs rosemary, leaves removed
and stems discarded
120 g feta cheese

Preheat the oven to 180°C (350°F/
Gas 4). Wrap each beetroot in foil
and place on a baking tray. Brush
the sweet potato with garlic oil and
season. Place on another baking tray
with the whole garlic bulb. Cook with
the beetroot for 35–40 minutes, or
until tender. Test with a skewer, and
when tender, remove from the oven
and allow to cool.

Heat 1 tablespoon of olive oil and
the butter in a small saucepan over
medium heat until the butter has
melted. Add the onion and cook,
stirring occasionally, for 15 minutes,
or until soft. Add the vinegar and
sugar, and cook for 3–5 minutes,
or until the onion is golden and
starting to caramelise.

Peel the garlic cloves and combine
them with the lemon juice, basil and
remaining oil. Season to taste.

Toss the spinach, beetroot, sweet
potato, onion and rosemary in a bowl.
Crumble the feta over the top and
drizzle with the dressing. Serve warm.

Serves 4

Note: If garlic oil is unavailable, you
may make your own by steeping
some crushed garlic in extra virgin
olive oil for 2 hours, then straining,
or use plain olive oil.

Caponata

1 kg eggplant (aubergine), cubed
185 ml (¾ cup) olive oil
200 g zucchini (courgettes), cubed
1 red capsicum (pepper), thinly sliced
2 onions, finely sliced
4 celery stalks, sliced
400 g tin crushed tomatoes
3 tablespoons red wine vinegar
2 tablespoons sugar
2 tablespoons capers, rinsed
  and drained
24 green olives, pitted
2 tablespoons pine nuts, toasted

Put the eggplant in a colander, add 2 teaspoons of salt and leave to drain.

Heat 3 tablespoons of the oil in a large frying pan and fry the zucchini and capsicum for 5–6 minutes, or until the zucchini is lightly browned. Transfer to a bowl. Add a little more oil to the pan and gently fry the onion and celery for 6–8 minutes, or until softened but not brown. Transfer to the bowl with the zucchini.

Rinse the eggplant and pat dry. Add 60 ml (¼ cup) of the oil to the pan, increase the heat and brown the eggplant in batches. Keep adding more oil to each batch. Drain on paper towels and set aside.

Remove any excess oil from the pan and return the vegetables to the pan, except the eggplant.

Add 60 ml (¼ cup) water and the tomatoes. Reduce the heat and simmer for 10 minutes. Add the remaining ingredients and eggplant and mix well. Remove from the heat and cool. Cover and leave for 24 hours in the refrigerator. Add some pepper, and more vinegar if needed.

Serves 8

Frisée and garlic crouton salad

Vinaigrette
1 French shallot, finely chopped
1 tablespoon Dijon mustard
60 ml (¼ cup) tarragon vinegar
170 ml (⅔ cup) extra virgin olive oil

1 tablespoon olive oil
250 g speck, rind removed, cut into
   5 mm x 2 cm pieces
½ baguette, sliced
4 garlic cloves
1 baby frisée (curly endive), washed
   and dried
100 g (½ cup) walnuts, toasted

For the vinaigrette, whisk together in a bowl the shallot, mustard and vinegar. Slowly add the oil, whisking constantly until thickened. Set aside.

Heat the oil in a large frying pan, add the speck, bread and garlic cloves and cook over medium–high heat for 5–8 minutes, until the bread and speck are both crisp. Remove the garlic from the pan.

Place the frisée, bread, speck, walnuts and vinaigrette in a large bowl. Toss together well and serve.

Serves 4–6

Sweets

Baked lemon cheesecake

100 g plain sweet biscuits, crushed
75 g butter, melted
300 g low-fat ricotta cheese
200 g light cream cheese
125 g (½ cup) caster sugar
80 ml (⅓ cup) lemon juice
2 tablespoons grated lemon zest
1 egg
1 egg white

Preheat the oven to 160°C (315°F/ Gas 2–3). Lightly grease an 18 cm springform tin and line the base with baking paper. Combine the crushed biscuits and butter and press into the base of the tin. Refrigerate for 30 minutes.

Beat the ricotta, cream cheese, sugar, lemon juice and 3 teaspoons of lemon zest with electric beaters until smooth. Beat in the egg and egg white.

Pour the mixture into the tin and sprinkle the surface with the remaining lemon zest. Bake for 45 minutes — the centre will still be a little wobbly. Leave to cool, then chill for 5 hours before serving.

Serves 8

Orchard fruit compote

90 g (¼ cup) honey
½ teaspoon ground ginger
1 cinnamon stick
3 whole cloves
pinch ground nutmeg
750 ml (3 cups) dessert wine
   such as Sauternes
1 lemon
6 pitted prunes
3 dried peaches, halved
5 dates, seeded and halved
10 dried apricots
1 lapsang souchong tea bag
2 golden delicious apples
2 beurre bosc pears
400 g Greek-style plain yoghurt

Place the honey, ginger, cinnamon stick, cloves, nutmeg and wine in a saucepan. Peel a large piece of zest from the lemon and place in the pan. Squeeze the juice from the lemon to give 60 ml (¼ cup) and add to the pan. Bring to the boil, stirring, then simmer for 20 minutes.

Meanwhile, place the prunes, peaches, dates and apricots in a large heatproof bowl. Cover with boiling water, add the tea bag and leave to soak. Peel and core the apples and pears, and cut into pieces about the same size as the dried fruits. Add to the syrup and allow to simmer for 8–10 minutes, or until tender. Drain the dried fruit and remove the tea bag, then add the fruit to the pan and cook for a further 5 minutes.

Remove all the fruit from the pan with a slotted spoon and place in a serving dish. Return the pan to the heat, bring to the boil, then reduce the heat and simmer for 6 minutes, or until the syrup has reduced by half. Pour over the fruit compote and chill for 30 minutes. Serve with the yoghurt.

Serves 4

Berries in Champagne jelly

1 litre Champagne or sparkling white
  wine
1½ tablespoons gelatine
250 g (1 cup) sugar
4 strips lemon zest
4 strips orange zest
250 g (1⅔ cups) small hulled and
  halved strawberries
255 g (1⅔ cups) blueberries

Pour 500 ml (2 cups) Champagne into a bowl and let the bubbles subside. Sprinkle the gelatine over the Champagne in an even layer. Leave until the gelatine is spongy — do not stir. Place the remaining Champagne in a large saucepan with the sugar, lemon and orange zest, and heat gently, stirring constantly for 3–4 minutes, or until all of the sugar has dissolved.

Remove the pan from the heat, add the gelatine mixture and stir until thoroughly dissolved. Leave the jelly to cool completely, then remove the lemon and orange zest.

Divide the berries among eight 125 ml (½ cup) stemmed wine glasses and gently pour the jelly over the top. Refrigerate for 6 hours or overnight, or until the jelly has fully set. Remove from the refrigerator 15 minutes before serving.

Serves 8

Macaroon berry trifle

420 ml (1²/₃ cups) skim milk
2 tablespoons caster sugar
1 teaspoon natural vanilla essence
2½ tablespoons custard powder
1 tablespoon Marsala
2 teaspoons instant coffee powder
16 amaretti biscuits, roughly broken
2 tablespoons orange juice
200 g fresh raspberries
425 g tin pears in natural juice,
   drained, roughly chopped

vanilla ice cream

Place the milk, sugar and vanilla in a heavy-based saucepan and cook over low heat, stirring occasionally. Combine the custard powder with 2 tablespoons of water, mix to a smooth paste and whisk into the milk mixture until the custard boils and thickens. Remove from the heat and cover with plastic wrap, placing it directly on the surface of the custard to prevent any skin forming, and allow to cool.

Place the Marsala and coffee powder in a small bowl and stir until the coffee has dissolved. Place the biscuits and orange juice in a large bowl and stir to coat the biscuits. Layer half of the biscuit in the base of four serving glasses and drizzle with the Marsala mixture. Top with a third of the berries and half of the pear, then pour in half of the custard. Repeat the layering, finishing with the raspberries. Refrigerate the trifles for 10 minutes or serve immediately with a scoop of vanilla ice cream.

Serves 4

Chocolate and raspberry ice cream sandwich

300 g frozen chocolate pound cake
2 tablespoons raspberry liqueur, optional
250 g (2 cups) fresh or thawed raspberries
250 g (1 cup) sugar
1 teaspoon lemon juice
1 litre vanilla ice cream, softened
icing sugar, to dust

Using a sharp knife, cut the pound cake lengthwise into four thin slices. Using a 6.5 cm plain cutter, cut eight rounds from the slices of cake. You will need two rounds of cake per person. Brush each round with half of the raspberry liqueur if using, then cover and set aside.

Line a 20 x 20 cm tin or dish with baking paper, leaving a generous overhang of paper on two opposite sides. Place the raspberries, sugar, lemon juice and remaining liqueur in a blender and blend to a smooth purée. Reserving 125 ml (½ cup) of the purée, fold the remainder through the ice cream and pour into the tin. Freeze for 2 hours, or until firm.

Remove the ice cream from the freezer and use the overhanging baking paper to lift from the tin. Using a 6.5 cm cutter, cut four rounds from the ice cream.

To assemble, place four slices of cake on a tray, top each with a round of ice cream and then the remaining slices of cake. Smooth the sides of the ice cream to neaten, if necessary. Return the sandwiches to the freezer for 5 minutes to firm. Dust with icing sugar and serve with the remaining raspberry sauce.

Serves 4

Mango sorbet

375 g (1½ cups) caster sugar
125 ml (½ cup) lime juice
5 fresh mangoes (1.5 kg)

Place the sugar in a saucepan with 625 ml (2½ cups) water. Stir over low heat until the sugar dissolves, then bring to the boil. Reduce to a simmer for 15 minutes, then stir in the juice.

Peel the mangoes and remove the flesh from the stone. Chop and place in a heatproof bowl. Add the syrup and leave to cool.

Place the mango mixture in a blender, blend until smooth, then pour into a shallow metal dish and freeze for 1 hour, or until it starts to freeze around the edges. Return to the blender and blend until smooth. Pour back into the tray and return to the freezer. Repeat three times. For the final freezing, place in an airtight container and cover the sorbet with a piece of greaseproof paper and lid. Allow the sorbet to soften slightly before serving with tropical fruit.

Serves 4

Note: You can use frozen mango if fresh is unavailable. Use 1 kg frozen mango cheeks, softened, 185 g (¾ cup) caster sugar and 60 ml (¼ cup) lime juice, and follow the method as above.

Lemon grass and ginger infused fruit salad

60 g (¼ cup) caster sugar
2 cm x 2 cm piece fresh ginger, thinly
   sliced
1 stalk lemon grass, bruised and
   halved
1 large passionfruit
1 red pawpaw
½ honeydew melon
1 large mango
1 small fresh pineapple
12 fresh lychees
5 g (¼ cup) mint leaves, shredded

Place the sugar, ginger and lemon grass in a small saucepan, add 125 ml (½ cup) water and stir over low heat to dissolve the sugar. Boil for 5 minutes, or until reduced to 80 ml (⅓ cup) and cool. Strain the syrup and add the passionfruit pulp.

Peel and seed the pawpaw and melon. Cut into 4 cm cubes. Peel the mango and cut the flesh into cubes, discarding the stone. Peel, halve and core the pineapple and cut into cubes. Peel the lychees, then make a slit in the flesh and remove the seed.

Place all the fruit in a large serving bowl. Pour on the syrup, or serve separately if preferred. Garnish with the shredded mint.

Serves 4

Choc-chip banana ice

600 ml ready-made low-fat custard
2 ripe bananas, mashed
2 teaspoons lemon juice
50 g dark chocolate

Combine the custard, mashed banana and lemon juice in a large mixing bowl. Beat with electric beaters until the banana and custard are well combined, with no lumps of banana remaining.

Pour into a metal cake tin, cover with plastic wrap and freeze for 3–4 hours, or until semi-frozen. Transfer to a chilled bowl and beat for 2 minutes with electric beaters until slushy, then return to the cake tin and place in the freezer for 2–3 hours, or until almost firm. Repeat the freezing and beating twice more (for a total of three times).

Finely chop the chocolate and fold into the mixture after the last beating. Refreeze in an airtight plastic container. Remove from the freezer and allow the ice cream to soften slightly before serving.

Serves 6

Cassata

30 g crystallised ginger, finely
   chopped
50 g red glacé cherries, roughly
   chopped or sliced
300 g low-fat vanilla ice cream,
   softened
250 g frozen strawberry fruit dessert,
   softened
300 g low-fat chocolate ice cream,
   softened

Line a 1.25 litre rectangular tin with plastic wrap, leaving an overhang on the sides.

Stir the ginger and glacé cherries into the vanilla ice cream until well combined. Spoon into the prepared tin and smooth down. Freeze for 1 hour, or until firm.

Spoon the strawberry fruit dessert over the ice cream mixture, smooth the surface and return to the freezer for another hour.

Spoon the chocolate ice cream over the strawberry, smoothing the surface. Cover with plastic wrap, and freeze for at least 3 hours or overnight. To serve, plunge the bottom of the tin into warm water for 10 seconds to loosen and lift out using the plastic wrap. Cut into slices and serve.

Serves 10–12

Summer pudding

150 g blackcurrants
150 g redcurrants
150 g raspberries
150 g blackberries
200 g strawberries, hulled and
  quartered or halved
125 g (½ cup) caster sugar, or
  to taste
6–8 slices good-quality sliced white
  bread, crusts removed

Put all the berries except the strawberries in a saucepan with 125 ml (½ cup) water and heat for 5 minutes, or until the berries begin to soften. Add the strawberries and remove from the heat. Add sugar, to taste (how much you need will depend on how ripe the fruit is). Cool.

Line six 170 ml (⅔ cup) moulds or a 1 litre pudding basin with the bread. For the small moulds cut a circle to fit the bottom and strips to fit around the sides. For the basin, cut a large circle out of one slice for the bottom and cut the rest of the bread into strips to fit the side. Drain a little of the juice off the fruit. Dip one side of each piece of bread in the juice before fitting it, juice-side-down, into the basin, leaving no gaps. Do not squeeze the bread or it will not absorb the juice.

Fill each mould with fruit and add some juice. Cover the top with the remaining dipped bread, juice-side up. Cover with plastic wrap. For the small moulds, sit a small tin on top of each. For the basin, sit a small plate onto the plastic wrap, then weigh it down with a large tin. Place on a tray to catch any juice which may overflow, and chill overnight. Carefully turn out the pudding and serve with leftover fruit mixture and cream if desired.

Serves 6

White chocolate mousse

100 g white chocolate melts (buttons)
125 ml (½ cup) skim milk
2 teaspoons gelatine
400 g low-fat French vanilla fromage
  frais or whipped yoghurt
3 egg whites
3 tablespoons passionfruit pulp
icing sugar, to dust

Place the chocolate and milk in a small saucepan and stir over low heat until the chocolate has melted. Allow to cool. Place 60 ml (¼ cup) boiling water in a heatproof bowl, sprinkle evenly with the gelatine, and stir until dissolved. Using a wooden spoon, stir the gelatine into the chocolate mixture.

Place the fromage frais in a large bowl and gradually stir in the chocolate mixture, a little at a time, stirring until smooth after each addition.

Beat the egg whites in a clean, dry bowl with electric beaters until soft peaks form. Gently fold the egg whites and the passionfruit pulp into the chocolate mixture. Divide the mixture equally among eight 125 ml (½ cup) serving dishes or a 1 litre glass bowl. Refrigerate for 3 hours, or until set. Serve with a light dusting of icing sugar.

Serves 8

Note: It is important to have the ingredients at room temperature to ensure the texture is smooth.

Watermelon granita

250 g (1 cup) caster sugar
1.5 kg watermelon

Place the sugar in a saucepan with 250 ml (1 cup) water and stir over low heat without boiling until the sugar has completely dissolved. Increase the heat and bring to the boil, then reduce the heat and simmer, without stirring, for 5 minutes. Pour into a large bowl to cool.

Remove the rind from the watermelon and place chunks of flesh in a food processor. Process until puréed, then strain to remove the seeds and fibre. Mix the watermelon purée with the sugar syrup, and pour into a shallow metal dish. Freeze for 1 hour, or until just frozen around the edges. Scrape this back into the mixture with a fork.

Repeat scraping the frozen edges every hour, at least twice more, or until the mixture has even-sized ice crystals. Serve immediately or beat well with a fork and refreeze just before serving. To serve, scrape the granita into serving dishes with a fork, or serve in scoops in a tall glass.

Serves 4

Variation: For refreshing extra flavour, add 2 tablespoons chopped mint when freezing the last time.

Almond semifreddo

300 ml cream
4 eggs, at room temperature,
    separated
85 g (2/3 cup) icing sugar
60 ml (1/4 cup) Amaretto
80 g (1/2 cup) blanched almonds,
    toasted and chopped
8 amaretti biscuits, crushed

fresh fruit or extra Amaretto

Whip the cream until firm peaks form, cover and chill. Line a 10 x 21 cm loaf tin with plastic wrap so that it overhangs the two long sides.

Place the egg yolks and icing sugar in a large bowl and beat until pale and creamy. Whisk the egg whites in a separate bowl until firm peaks form. Stir the Amaretto, almonds and amaretti biscuits into the egg yolk mixture, then carefully fold in the chilled cream and the egg whites until well combined. Carefully pour or spoon into the lined loaf tin and cover with the overhanging plastic. Freeze for 4 hours, or until frozen but not rock hard. Serve in slices with fresh fruit or a sprinkling of Amaretto. The semifreddo can also be poured into individual moulds or serving dishes before freezing.

Serves 8–10

Note: Semifreddo means semi-frozen, so if you want to leave it in the freezer overnight, remove it and place it in the refrigerator for 30 minutes to soften slightly before serving.

Petite custard tarts

3 sheets ready-made shortcrust
   pastry
250 ml (1 cup) skim milk
1 tablespoon custard powder
60 g (1/4 cup) caster sugar
1 teaspoon vanilla essence
80 ml (1/3 cup) passionfruit pulp
1/2 teaspoon gelatine powder

Preheat the oven to 180°C (350°F/
Gas 4). Cut 12 circles from the pastry
sheets using an 8 cm round cutter.
Gently press into 12 patty tins (6 cm
diameter x 2.5 cm deep) and prick
each round with a fork.

Cut out a 5 cm square of foil for each
case and press into the pastry cases.
Bake for 10 minutes, remove the foil
and bake for 5 minutes, or until golden
and cooked through. Cool on a rack.

Mix 1 tablespoon of the milk and the
custard powder until smooth. Stir the
sugar, vanilla and remaining milk over
medium heat for 1 minute, or until
the sugar dissolves. Stir in the
custard mixture and cook, stirring,
for 2–3 minutes, or until thick. Cover
the surface of the custard with plastic
wrap. Cool to room temperature.

Place the passionfruit in a heatproof
bowl and sprinkle with gelatine. Leave
until the gelatine is spongy. Bring a
saucepan of water to the boil, remove
from the heat and place the bowl
in the pan. Stir until the gelatine
dissolves, then leave to cool. Divide
the custard among the pastry cases.
Top each with 1 teaspoon of the
passionfruit glaze and chill for at
least 2 hours.

Makes 12

Individual zucotto

450 g packet Madeira cake
60 ml (¼ cup) Cointreau
60 ml (¼ cup) brandy
300 ml thick (double) cream
3 teaspoons icing sugar, sifted
80 g (½ cup) blanched almonds,
  roasted, roughly chopped
70 g (½ cup) hazelnuts, roasted,
  roughly chopped
150 g good-quality dark chocolate,
  finely chopped

Cut the cake into 5 mm slices. Lightly grease six 150 ml ramekins and line with plastic wrap, leaving enough to hang over the sides. Press the pieces of the cake into the ramekins, overlapping to cover the base and sides. Combine the Cointreau and brandy in a bowl. Brush the cake with half the Cointreau mixture.

Place the cream and icing sugar in a bowl, and, using electric beaters, beat until firm and stiff. Fold in the nuts, chocolate and 1½ teaspoons Cointreau mixture. The mixture will be quite stiff.

Spoon the mixture into each ramekin and smooth over the surface. Cover with the overhanging plastic wrap and refrigerate for 2 hours or overnight. To serve, use the plastic wrap to lift the zucotto out of the ramekins, turn upside-down onto serving plates and brush with the remaining Cointreau mixture.

Serves 6

Apple and pear sorbet

4 large green apples, peeled, cored
  and chopped
4 pears, peeled, cored and chopped
1 piece of lemon zest (1.5 cm x 4 cm)
1 cinnamon stick
60 ml (¼ cup) lemon juice
4 tablespoons caster sugar
2 tablespoons Calvados or poire
  William liqueur, optional

Place the apple and pear in a large deep saucepan with the lemon zest, cinnamon stick and enough water to just cover the fruit. Cover and poach the fruit gently over medium–low heat for 6–8 minutes, or until tender. Remove the lemon zest and cinnamon stick. Place the fruit in a food processor and blend with the lemon juice until smooth.

Place the sugar in a saucepan with 80 ml (⅓ cup) water, bring to the boil and simmer for 1 minute. Add the fruit purée and the liqueur and combine.

Pour into a shallow metal tray and freeze for 2 hours, or until the mixture is frozen around the edges. Transfer to a food processor or bowl and blend or beat until just smooth. Pour back into the tray and return to the freezer. Repeat this process three times. For the final freezing, place in an airtight container, cover the surface with a piece of greaseproof paper and cover with a lid. Serve in small glasses or bowls.

Serves 4–6

Notes: Pour an extra nip of Calvados over the sorbet to serve, if desired.

Spiced poached pears

6 beurre bosc pears
300 ml rosé wine
150 ml good-quality apple or pear
  juice
4 cloves
1 vanilla bean, halved
1 cinnamon stick
1 tablespoon maple syrup
200 g low-fat vanilla yoghurt

Peel, halve and core the pears. Place in a deep frying pan with a lid, and add the wine, fruit juice and cloves. Scrape the seeds out of the vanilla bean and add both the seeds and pod to the pan. Stir in the cinnamon stick and maple syrup. Bring to the boil, then reduce the heat and simmer for 5–7 minutes, or until the pears are tender. Remove from the heat and cover with the lid.

Leave the fruit for 30 minutes to allow the flavours to infuse, then remove the pears with a slotted spoon and place in a serving dish. Return the syrup to the heat and boil for 6–8 minutes, or until reduced by half. Strain the syrup over the pears. Serve warm or chilled with the yoghurt.

Serves 6

Ginger and lychee jelly

565 g tin lychees
500 ml (2 cups) clear apple juice
  (no added sugar)
80 ml (⅓ cup) strained lime juice
2 tablespoons caster sugar
3 cm x 3 cm piece fresh ginger,
  peeled and thinly sliced
4 sheets gelatine (about 5 g)

mint leaves

Drain the syrup from the lychees and reserve 250 ml (1 cup) of the syrup. Discard the remaining syrup. Place the reserved syrup, apple juice, lime juice, sugar and ginger in a saucepan. Bring to the boil, then reduce the heat and simmer for 5 minutes. Strain into a heatproof bowl.

Place the gelatine sheets in a bowl of cold water and soak for 2 minutes, or until they soften. Squeeze out the excess water, then add to the syrup. Stir until the gelatine has completely dissolved. Leave to cool.

Pour 2 tablespoons of the jelly mixture into each of six 150 ml stemmed wine glasses, and divide the lychees among the wine glasses. Refrigerate until the jelly has set. Spoon the remaining jelly over the fruit and refrigerate until set. Before serving, garnish with mint leaves.

Serves 6

Peaches poached in wine

4 just-ripe yellow-fleshed freestone
  peaches
500 ml (2 cups) dessert wine such
  as Sauternes
60 ml (1/4 cup) orange liqueur
250 g (1 cup) sugar
1 cinnamon stick
1 vanilla bean, split
8 mint leaves

mascarpone cheese or crème fraîche

Cut a small cross in the base of each peach. Immerse the peaches in boiling water for 30 seconds, then drain and cool slightly. Peel off the skin, cut in half and carefully remove the stones.

Place the wine, liqueur, sugar, cinnamon stick and vanilla bean in a deep-sided frying pan large enough to hold the peach halves in a single layer. Heat the mixture, stirring, until the sugar dissolves. Bring to the boil, then reduce the heat and simmer for 5 minutes. Add the peaches to the pan and simmer for 4 minutes, turning them over halfway through. Remove with a slotted spoon and leave to cool. Continue to simmer the syrup for 6–8 minutes, or until thick. Strain and set aside.

Arrange the peaches on a serving platter, cut-side-up. Spoon the syrup over the top and garnish each half with a mint leaf. Serve the peaches warm or chilled, with a dollop of mascarpone or crème fraîche.

Serves 4

Lemon granita

315 ml (1¼ cups) lemon juice
1 tablespoon lemon zest
200 g caster sugar

Place the lemon juice, lemon zest and caster sugar in a small saucepan and stir over low heat for 5 minutes, or until the sugar is dissolved. Remove from the heat and leave to cool.

Add 500 ml (2 cups) water to the juice mixture and mix together well. Pour the mixture into a shallow 30 x 20 cm metal container and place in the freezer until the mixture is beginning to freeze around the edges. Scrape the frozen sections back into the mixture with a fork. Repeat every 30 minutes until the mixture has even-size ice crystals. Beat the mixture with a fork just before serving. To serve, spoon the lemon granita into six chilled glasses.

Serves 6

Pannacotta with blueberry compote

300 ml low-fat milk
1 vanilla bean, halved
1 cinnamon stick
1/2 teaspoon vanilla essence
1 tablespoon caster sugar
2 sheets gelatine
200 g plain yoghurt

Blueberry compote
150 g fresh blueberries
15 g caster sugar
100 ml good-quality Marsala
1 cinnamon stick
2 cm strip lemon peel, white pith
  removed
1/2 vanilla bean, halved
1/2 teaspoon arrowroot

Pour the milk into a heavy-based saucepan. Scrape in the seeds from the vanilla bean and add the pod, cinnamon stick, vanilla essence and the sugar. Bring to the boil, stirring, then remove from the heat and leave to infuse for 10 minutes.

Soak the gelatine in cold water for 5 minutes, or until soft. Squeeze out and add the leaves to the milk. Stir over low heat until the leaves dissolve (do not boil). Remove the vanilla pod and the cinnamon stick. Cool to room temperature. Whisk in the yoghurt. Pour into four 125 ml (1/2 cup) ramekins and chill for 6 hours, or until set.

Place the berries in a saucepan and add the sugar, Marsala, cinnamon stick and peel. Scrape in the seeds from the vanilla bean and add the pod. Cook over low heat for 15 minutes, stirring occasionally. Make sure the fruit does not break up. Mix the arrowroot with 2 teaspoons water and add to the fruit. Cook, stirring, until the mixture thickens. Leave to cool for at least 2 hours.

Run a knife around the edge of each ramekin and invert the pannacotta onto plates. Remove the cinnamon, peel and pod from the compote, and serve with the pannacotta.

Serves 4

Chocolate mousse

100 g dark chocolate
60 ml (¼ cup) evaporated skim milk
2 tablespoons cocoa powder
¼ teaspoon rosewater essence or
  2 teaspoons vanilla essence
125 g (½ cup) caster sugar
3 egg whites
cocoa powder, to dust

savoiardi (sponge finger biscuits)

Chop the chocolate into small, even pieces and place in a heatproof bowl with the milk and cocoa powder. Bring a saucepan of water to the boil, then reduce the heat to a gentle simmer. Sit the bowl over the saucepan, making sure the base of the bowl does not touch the water. Stir once, if necessary, to ensure even melting. When completely melted, mix until smooth, then stir in the rosewater essence and leave to cool.

Place the sugar and 80 ml (⅓ cup) water in a small, heavy-based saucepan, and stir over low heat until the sugar has dissolved. Bring to a simmer, without stirring, for 5 minutes, or until a small amount of the syrup placed in a saucer of water forms a soft ball. Remove from the heat.

Meanwhile, using electric beaters, beat the egg whites in a clean, dry bowl until soft peaks form. With the beater on medium, gradually add the hot sugar syrup, then beat on high speed for 3–4 minutes, or until the meringue is very thick and glossy. Gently fold in the cooled chocolate mixture, then pour into four 160 ml serving glasses. Chill for at least 4 hours. Dust with cocoa and serve with a sponge finger biscuit.

Serves 4

Drinks

Earl Grey summer tea

1 cinnamon stick
1 tablespoon Earl Grey tea leaves
250 ml (1 cup) orange juice
2 teaspoons finely grated orange zest
2 tablespoons sugar, to taste
ice cubes
1 orange, sliced into thin rounds

4 cinnamon sticks

Place the cinnamon stick, tea leaves, orange juice, orange zest and 750 ml (3 cups) water in a medium pan.

Slowly bring to a simmer over gentle heat. Once simmering, stir in the sugar, to taste, and stir until dissolved. Remove from the heat and allow to cool. Once the mixture has cooled, strain the liquid into a jug and refrigerate until cold.

Serve in a jug with lots of ice cubes, and garnish with the orange slices and extra cinnamon stick.

Makes 4 x 250 ml glasses

Lemon, lime and soda with citrus ice cubes

1 lemon
1 lime
2½ tablespoons lemon juice
170 ml (²/₃ cup) lime juice cordial
625 ml (2½ cups) soda water, chilled

Using a sharp knife, remove the peel and white pith from the lemon and lime. On a chopping board, cut between the membranes to release the segments. Place a lemon and lime segment in each hole of an ice cube tray and cover with water. Freeze for 2–3 hours or overnight until firm.

Combine the lemon juice, lime juice cordial and soda water.

Pour into long, chilled glasses with the ice cubes.

Makes 2 x 375 ml glasses and 8 ice cubes

Passionfruit and vanilla ice cream whip

4 passionfruit
100 g passionfruit yoghurt
500 ml (2 cups) milk
1 tablespoon caster sugar
2 scoops vanilla ice cream

Scoop out the pulp from the passionfruit and push through a sieve to remove the seeds. Place into the blender with the yoghurt, milk, sugar and ice cream and blend until smooth.

Pour into tall glasses and serve with an extra scoop of ice cream, if desired.

Makes 2 x 375 ml glasses

Melon shake

500 g rockmelon, peeled and seeded
2 tablespoons honey
375 ml (1½ cups) milk
5 scoops vanilla ice cream

ground nutmeg

Cut the rockmelon into 2 cm pieces and place in a blender. Mix for 30 seconds, or until smooth.

Add the honey, milk and ice cream and blend the mixture for a further 10–20 seconds, or until well combined and smooth. Serve sprinkled with nutmeg.

Makes 2 x 375 ml glasses

Coconut and lime lassi

400 ml coconut milk
185 g (3/4 cup) plain yoghurt
60 ml (1/4 cup) lime juice
60 g (1/4 cup) caster sugar
8–10 ice cubes

lime slices

Blend together the coconut milk, yoghurt, lime juice, sugar and ice cubes until the mixture is well combined and the ice cubes are well crushed.

Pour into tall glasses and serve immediately, garnished with slices of fresh lime.

Makes 2 x 375 ml glasses

Peachy egg nog

2 eggs, separated
60 ml (¼ cup) milk
60 g (¼ cup) caster sugar
80 ml (⅓ cup) cream
440 ml (1¾ cups) peach nectar
2 tablespoons orange juice

ground nutmeg

Beat the egg yolks, milk and half the sugar in a bowl and place over a pan of simmering water — do not allow the base of the bowl to touch the water. Cook, stirring, for 8 minutes, or until the custard thickens. Remove from the heat and cover the surface with plastic wrap. Cool.

Beat the egg whites until frothy. Add the remaining sugar, to taste, then beat until stiff peaks form. In a separate bowl, whip the cream until soft peaks form.

Gently fold the egg whites and cream into the cooled custard. Stir in the nectar and juice. Cover and chill for 2 hours.

Beat the mixture lightly, pour into glasses and sprinkle with nutmeg.

Makes 4 x 225 ml glasses

Cranberry and vanilla ice cream spider

500 ml (2 cups) cranberry juice
500 ml (2 cups) soda water
4 scoops vanilla ice cream
185 ml (¾ cup) cream
1 tablespoon caster sugar
20 g flaked almonds, toasted

Combine the juice and soda water in a jug. Add a scoop of ice cream to each tall glass. Pour the juice and soda over the ice cream.

Whip the cream and sugar until soft peaks form. Spoon over the juice and soda and top with a sprinkle of almonds.

Makes 4 x 250 ml glasses

Summer buttermilk smoothie

350 g rockmelon
2 peaches, peeled and sliced
150 g strawberries, roughly chopped
4 mint leaves
125 ml (½ cup) buttermilk
125 ml (½ cup) orange juice
1–2 tablespoons honey

Remove the zest and seeds from the melon and cut the flesh into pieces.

Place the rockmelon, peaches, strawberries and mint leaves in a blender and blend until smooth.

Add the buttermilk, orange juice and 1 tablespoon of the honey and blend to combine. Taste for sweetness and add more honey if needed.

Makes 2 x 375 ml glasses

Note: This drink should be consumed within 3 hours of being made or it will lose colour and freshness of flavour.

Blackcurrant crush

750 ml (3 cups) apple and
  blackcurrant juice
500 ml (2 cups) soda water
1 tablespoon caster sugar
150 g blueberries
ice cubes

Place the apple and blackcurrant juice, soda water, sugar and blueberries into a blender and blend until smooth.

Serve in chilled glasses over ice.

Makes 4 x 300 ml glasses

Note: If you have a really good blender, you may wish to add the ice cubes when blending the other ingredients to make a slushy.

Apricot whip

75 g dried apricots
125 g (½ cup) apricot yoghurt
170 ml (⅔ cup) light coconut milk
315 ml (1¼ cups) milk
1 tablespoon honey
1 scoop vanilla ice cream

flaked coconut, toasted

Cover the apricots with boiling water and soak for 15 minutes. Drain and roughly chop. Place the apricots, yoghurt, coconut milk, milk, honey and ice cream in a blender and blend until smooth.

Pour into tall, chilled glasses and sprinkle with the flaked coconut.

Makes 3 x 250 ml glasses

Chocoholic thickshake

125 ml (½ cup) cold milk
50 g dark chocolate, grated
2 tablespoons chocolate syrup
2 tablespoons cream
4 scoops chocolate ice cream
2 scoops chocolate ice cream, extra

grated dark chocolate

Blend the milk, chocolate, syrup, cream and ice cream in a blender until smooth.

Pour into chilled glasses. Top each glass with a scoop of ice cream and sprinkle with grated chocolate.

Makes 2 x 250 ml glasses

Banana date smoothie

250 g (1 cup) low-fat plain yoghurt
125 ml (½ cup) skim milk
50 g (½ cup) fresh dates, stoned
  and chopped
2 bananas, sliced
8 ice cubes

Place the yoghurt, milk, dates,
banana and ice cubes in a blender.
Blend until the mixture is smooth
and the ice cubes have been well
incorporated.

Serve in chilled glasses.

Makes 2 x 350 ml glasses

Orange and cardamom herbal tea

3 cardamom pods
250 ml (1 cup) orange juice
3 strips orange zest
2 tablespoons caster sugar

Place the cardamom pods on a chopping board and press with the side of a large knife to crack them open. Place the cardamom, orange juice, zest, sugar and 500 ml (2 cups) water in a pan and stir over medium heat for 10 minutes, or until the sugar has dissolved. Bring to the boil then remove from the heat.

Leave to infuse for 2–3 hours, or until cold. Chill in the refrigerator. Strain and serve over ice.

Makes 2 x 275 ml glasses

Virgin Mary

750 ml (3 cups) tomato juice
2 tablespoons lemon juice
1 tablespoon Worcestershire sauce
1/4 teaspoon ground nutmeg
few drops Tabasco sauce
1 cup ice (12 ice cubes)
2 lemon slices, halved

Place the tomato juice, lemon juice, Worcestershire sauce, nutmeg and Tabasco sauce in a large jug and stir until combined.

Place the ice cubes in a blender and blend for 30 seconds, or until the ice is crushed down to 1/2 cup.

Pour the tomato juice mixture into serving glasses and add the crushed ice and lemon slices. Season with salt and pepper before serving.

Makes 4 x 200 ml glasses

Mandarin and mango chill

1 mango, cut into slices
500 ml (2 cups) mandarin juice
125 ml (½ cup) lime juice cordial
375 ml (1½ cups) soda water
2 tablespoons caster sugar
ice cubes

Freeze the mango for about 1 hour, or until semi-frozen.

Combine the juice, cordial, soda water and sugar in a jug.

Place the mango slices and some ice cubes into each glass, then pour in the juice mix.

Makes 2 x 375 ml glasses

Very berry

250 g (1 cup) low-fat strawberry
  yoghurt
125 ml (½ cup) cranberry juice, chilled
250 g strawberries, hulled and
  quartered
125 g frozen raspberries

Combine the yoghurt and cranberry juice in a blender. Add the quartered strawberries and 80 g of the raspberries. Blend until smooth.

Pour into chilled glasses and top with the remaining frozen raspberries. Serve with a spoon as it is quite thick.

Makes 4 x 200 ml glasses

Summer strawberry smoothie

1 tablespoon strawberry flavouring
250 ml (1 cup) wildberry drinking
  yoghurt
250 g strawberries, hulled
4 scoops frozen strawberry yoghurt
few drops vanilla essence
ice cubes

Combine the strawberry flavouring,
drinking yoghurt, strawberries, frozen
yoghurt and vanilla in a blender and
process until smooth.

Pour over lots of ice to serve.

Makes 2 x 300 ml glasses

Big bold banana

750 ml (3 cups) soy milk, chilled
125 g soft silken tofu
4 very ripe bananas, sliced
1 tablespoon honey
1 tablespoon vanilla essence
1 tablespoon cocoa powder

Combine the soy milk and tofu in a blender. Add the banana, honey, vanilla essence and cocoa powder. Blend until smooth.

Serve in tall chilled glasses with a long spoon.

Makes 4 x 375 ml glasses

Orange and ginger tea cooler

1 small orange
½–1 tablespoon Darjeeling tea leaves
250 ml (1 cup) ginger beer
8 thin slices glacé ginger
2 tablespoons sugar
4–6 ice cubes

mint leaves

Remove the peel from the orange using a vegetable peeler, avoiding the white pith, and cut into long thin strips. Place half the peel and the tea leaves in a bowl and pour in 500 ml (2 cups) boiling water. Cover and leave to steep for 5 minutes, then strain through a fine strainer.

Pour into a jug, add the ginger beer and chill for 6 hours, or overnight if possible.

One hour before serving, add the ginger, sugar and remaining orange peel. Stir well.

Pour into tall glasses, add 2–3 ice cubes per glass and garnish with mint leaves.

Makes 2 x 375 ml glasses

Lemon barley water

110 g (½ cup) pearl barley
3 lemons
125 g (½ cup) caster sugar
crushed ice

lemon slices

Wash the barley well and place in a medium pan. Using a sharp vegetable peeler, remove the peel from the lemons, avoiding the bitter white pith. Squeeze out the juice and set aside. Add the peel and 1.75 litres cold water to the barley and bring to the boil. Simmer briskly for 30 minutes. Add the sugar and mix to dissolve. Allow to cool.

Strain the liquid into a jug and add the lemon juice. Serve over crushed ice and garnish with lemon slices.

Makes 4 x 250 ml glasses

Homemade lemonade

685 ml (2¾ cups) lemon juice
310 g (1¼ cups) sugar
ice cubes

mint leaves

Combine the lemon juice and sugar in a large bowl, stirring until the sugar has dissolved. Pour into a large jug.

Add 1.25 litres water to the jug, stirring well to combine. Chill.

To serve, pour over ice cubes and garnish with mint leaves.

Makes 6 x 375 ml glasses

Banana passion

3 passionfruit, halved
1 large banana, chopped
250 ml (1 cup) skim milk
60 g (¼ cup) low-fat plain yoghurt

Scoop out the passionfruit pulp and place in a blender. Add the banana, milk and yoghurt and blend, turning quickly on and off (or use the pulse button), until smooth and the seeds are finely chopped. (Add more milk if it is too thick.) Don't blend for too long or it will become very bubbly and increase in volume.

Makes 2 x 250 ml glasses

Smoothberry

150 g strawberries, hulled
60 g raspberries
200 g boysenberries
250 ml (1 cup) milk
3 scoops vanilla ice cream

Place the strawberries, raspberries, boysenberries, milk and ice cream in a blender and blend until smooth, then chill.

Pour into chilled glasses and serve.

Makes 4 x 200 ml glasses

Note: If boysenberries are unavailable, any other berry can be used.

Iced chocolate

2 tablespoons rich chocolate topping
375 ml (1½ cups) icy-cold milk
1 scoop vanilla ice cream

whipped cream
drinking chocolate

Pour the chocolate topping into a glass and swirl it around the sides. Fill with the cold milk and add the ice cream.

Serve with a big swirl of whipped cream and dust with drinking chocolate.

Makes 1 x 375 ml glass

Lemon grass tea

3 stalks lemon grass
2 slices lemon
3 teaspoons honey, or to taste

lemon slices

Prepare the lemon grass by removing the first two tough outer layers. For maximum flavour, only use the bottom one-third of the stalk (the white part). Slice thinly into rings. (You could use the remaining stalks as a garnish, if you like.)

Place the lemon grass in a jug and cover with 2½ cups (625 ml) boiling water. Add the lemon slices and cover. Allow to infuse and cool. When cooled to room temperature, strain. Add the honey, to taste. Place the tea in the refrigerator to chill.

To serve, pour the tea into two glasses with extra slices of lemon. Add ice, if desired.

Makes 2 x 310 ml glasses

Raspberry lemonade

300 g fresh or frozen raspberries,
  thawed
310 g (1¼ cups) sugar
500 ml (2 cups) lemon juice
ice cubes

mint leaves

Combine the raspberries and sugar
in a blender and blend until smooth.

Place a strong sieve over a large
bowl and push the mixture through to
remove the seeds. Discard the seeds.

Add the lemon juice and mix well.
Pour into a large jug and stir in
1.5 litres water, then chill.

To serve, pour over ice cubes and
garnish with mint leaves.

Makes 6 x 375 ml glasses

Coconut and passionfruit smoothie

140 ml coconut milk
250 ml (1 cup) milk
25 g (¼ cup) desiccated coconut
¼ teaspoon natural vanilla essence
3 scoops vanilla ice cream
170 g tin passionfruit pulp in syrup

Blend together the coconut milk, milk, coconut, vanilla, ice cream and half the passionfruit pulp until the mixture is smooth and fluffy.

Stir in the remaining pulp and serve immediately.

Makes 2 x 375 ml glasses

Sports shake

500 ml (2 cups) milk, chilled
2 tablespoons honey
2 eggs
½ teaspoon vanilla essence
1 tablespoon wheat germ
1 medium banana, sliced

Blend the milk, honey, eggs, vanilla, wheat germ and banana until smooth.

Chill well and serve.

Makes 2 x 250 ml glasses

Iced mint tea

4 peppermint tea bags
115 g (⅓ cup) honey
500 ml (2 cups) grapefruit juice
250 ml (1 cup) orange juice

mint sprigs

Place the tea bags in a large heatproof jug and pour in 750 ml (3 cups) boiling water. Allow to steep for 3 minutes, then remove and discard the bags. Stir in the honey and allow to cool.

Add the grapefruit and orange juice. Cover and chill in the refrigerator. Serve in glasses, garnished with mint.

Makes 6 x 250 ml glasses

Mint julep

20 g (1 cup) mint leaves
1 tablespoon sugar
1 tablespoon lemon juice
250 ml (1 cup) pineapple juice
250 ml (1 cup) ginger ale
ice cubes

mint leaves

Roughly chop the mint leaves and place in a heatproof jug with the sugar. Using a wooden spoon, bruise the mint. Add the lemon juice, pineapple juice and 125 ml (½ cup) boiling water. Mix well. Cover with plastic wrap and leave for 30 minutes.

Strain, then refrigerate until cold.

Just before serving, add the ginger ale and mix well. Serve in glasses over ice and garnish with mint leaves.

Makes 2 x 300 ml glasses

Breakfast shake

150 g fruit (passionfruit, mango,
 banana, peaches, strawberries,
 blueberries)
250 ml (1 cup) milk
2 teaspoons wheat germ
1 tablespoon honey
60 g (¼ cup) vanilla yoghurt
1 egg, optional
1 tablespoon malt powder

Blend all the ingredients in a blender
for 30–60 seconds, or until well
combined.

Pour into chilled glasses and serve
immediately.

Makes 2 x 325 ml glasses

American iced tea

4 Ceylon tea bags
2 tablespoons sugar
2 tablespoons lemon juice
375 ml (1½ cups) dark grape juice
500 ml (2 cups) orange juice
375 ml (1½ cups) ginger ale
ice cubes

lemon slices

Place the tea bags in a heatproof bowl with 1 litre boiling water. Leave for 3 minutes. Remove the bags and stir in the sugar. Cool.

Stir in the juices. Refrigerate until cold, then add the ginger ale. Serve over ice cubes with a slice of lemon.

Makes 8 x 250 ml glasses

Cinnamon and custard shake

375 ml (1½ cups) milk
185 ml (¾ cup) prepared custard
3 teaspoons honey
1½ teaspoons ground cinnamon
3 scoops vanilla ice cream

ground cinnamon

Blend together the milk, custard, honey, cinnamon and ice cream until smooth and fluffy.

Pour the shake into tall glasses, sprinkle with the extra cinnamon and serve immediately.

Makes 2 x 375 ml glasses

Choc cherry smoothie

500 ml (2 cups) milk
55 g (¼ cup) whole red glacé cherries
25 g (¼ cup) desiccated coconut
1 tablespoon chocolate topping
3 scoops chocolate ice cream

Blend together the milk, cherries, coconut, topping and ice cream until smooth and fluffy.

Pour into tall glasses and serve immediately.

Makes 2 x 375 ml glasses

Index

INDEX

INDEX

Photographers: Jon Bader, Craig Cranko, Joe Filshie, Scott Hawkins, Ian Hofstetter, Andre Martin, Rob Reichenfeld, Brett Stevens, Jon Paul Urizar

Food stylist: Anna-Marie Bruechert, Marie-Hélène Clauzon, Jane Collins, Sarah de Nardi, Georgina Dolling, Carolyn Fienberg, Cherise Koch, Michelle Norianto, Sarah O'Brien, Sally Parker, Maria Villegas

Food preparation: Alison Adams, Valli Little, Tracey Meharg, Kerrie Mullins, Briget Palmer, Kim Passenger, Justine Poole, Christine Sheppard, Angela Tregonning

Special thanks to Wheel & Barrow, Sydney, who supplied props and accessories for the cover and chapter openers.

Published by Murdoch Books Pty Limited

Designer: Michelle Cutler (internals); Marylouise Brammer (cover)
Photographers: Jared Fowler (chapter openers); Stuart Scott (cover)
Stylists: Cherise Koch; (chapter openers); Louise Bickle (cover)
Editor: Gordana Trifunovic Production: Elizabeth Malcolm

Chief Executive: Juliet Rogers
Publishing Director: Kay Scarlett
Commissioning Editor: Lynn Lewis
Senior Designer: Heather Menzies

National Library of Australia Cataloguing-in-Publication Data
Title: Cool food/editor, Lynn Lewis. ISBN 9781741965285 (pbk.)
Series: New chunky. Includes index. Subjects: Salads. Cookery. 641.83

Printed by 1010 Printing International Ltd
PRINTED IN CHINA
First printed 2003. This edition 2009.

For fan-forced ovens, set the oven temperature to 20°C (35°F) lower than indicated in the recipe.
We have used 20 ml tablespoon measures. IMPORTANT: Those who might be at risk from the effects
of salmonella poisoning (the elderly, pregnant women, young children and those suffering from immune
deficiency diseases) should consult their GP with any concerns about eating raw eggs.

Cover credits: White flower side plate, White Home. Purple Japanese bowl, Dinosaur Designs.
Dibbern plum soup plate and handtowel col 26, Beclau. Multi-coloured stripe fabric, Ici et la.
Iittala Piano fork, Design Mode International. Yellow spot and purple stripe print fabrics, Spotlight.
Front flap: Vintage floral print fabric, ebay.

A catalogue record for this book is available from the British Library.

Published by:
AUSTRALIA
Murdoch Books Pty Ltd
Pier 8/9, 23 Hickson Road,
Millers Point NSW 2000
Phone: + 61 (0) 2 8220 2000
Fax: + 61 (0) 2 8220 2558
www.murdochbooks.com.au

UK
Murdoch Books UK Ltd
Erico House, 6th Floor North,
93-99 Upper Richmond Rd,
Putney, London SW15 2TG
Phone: + 44 (0) 20 8785 5995
Fax: + 44 (0) 20 8785 5985
www.murdochbooks.co.uk